**DISEASES & DISORDERS**

# Hodgkin's Disease

## Titles in the Diseases and Disorders series include:

- Acne
- AIDS
- Allergies
- Alzheimer's Disease
- Anorexia and Bulimia
- Anthrax
- Arthritis
- Anxiety Disorders
- Asthma
- Attention Deficit Disorder
- Autism
- Bipolar Disorder
- Birth Defects
- Blindness
- Brain Tumors
- Breast Cancer
- Cerebral Palsy
- Chronic Fatigue Syndrome
- Cystic Fibrosis
- Deafness
- Diabetes
- Down Syndrome
- Dyslexia
- The Ebola Virus
- Epilepsy
- Fetal Alcohol Syndrome
- Flu
- Food Poisoning
- Growth Disorders
- Headaches
- Heart Disease
- Hemophilia
- Hepatitis
- Human Papillomavirus (HPV)
- Leukemia
- Lou Gehrig's Disease
- Lyme Disease
- Mad Cow Disease
- Malaria
- Malnutrition
- Measles and Rubella
- Meningitis
- Mental Retardation
- Multiple Sclerosis
- Muscular Dystrophy
- Obesity
- Ovarian Cancer
- Parkinson's Disease
- Phobias
- Prostate Cancer
- SARS
- Schizophrenia
- Sexually Transmitted Diseases
- Sleep Disorders
- Smallpox
- Strokes
- Teen Depression
- Tuberculosis
- West Nile Virus

# DISEASES & DISORDERS

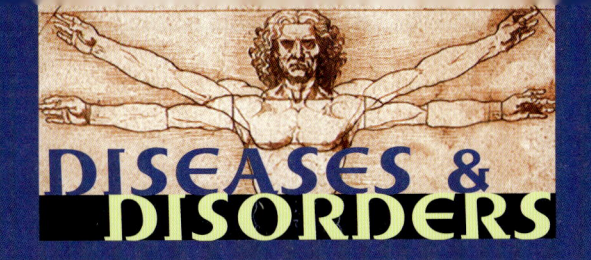

# Hodgkin's Disease

Sheila Wyborny

LUCENT BOOKS
*A part of Gale, Cengage Learning*

GALE
CENGAGE Learning

Detroit • New York • San Francisco • New Haven, Conn • Waterville, Maine • London

**GALE**
**CENGAGE Learning**

© 2009 Gale, Cengage Learning

ALL RIGHTS RESERVED. No part of this work covered by the copyright herein may be reproduced, transmitted, stored, or used in any form or by any means graphic, electronic, or mechanical, including but not limited to photocopying, recording, scanning, digitizing, taping, Web distribution, information networks, or information storage and retrieval systems, except as permitted under Section 107 or 108 of the 1976 United States Copyright Act, without the prior written permission of the publisher.

Every effort has been made to trace the owners of copyrighted material.

---

**LIBRARY OF CONGRESS CATALOGING-IN-PUBLICATION DATA**

Wyborny, Sheila, 1950 –
 Hodgkin's disease / by Sheila Wyborny.
  p. cm. — (Diseases & disorders)
 Includes bibliographical references and index.
 ISBN 978-1-59018-674-9 (hardcover)
 1. Hodgkin's disease—Juvenile literature. I. Title.
 RC644.W93 2009
 616.99'446—dc22

2008025705

---

Lucent Books
27500 Drake Rd.
Farmington Hills, MI 48331

ISBN-13: 978-1-59018-674-9
ISBN-10: 1-59018-674-5

Printed in the United States of America
1 2 3 4 5 6 7 12 11 10 09 08

# Table of Contents

**Foreword**   6

**Introduction**
Naming a Nightmare   8

**Chapter One**
What is Hodgkin's Disease?   14

**Chapter Two**
Diagnosing Hodgkin's Disease   26

**Chapter Three**
Treatments   39

**Chapter Four**
Alternative Therapies   52

**Chapter Five**
Living and Coping   65

**Chapter Six**
Today's Cutting Edge and Looking Ahead   77

**Notes**   89
**Glossary**   91
**Organizations to Contact**   93
**For Further Reading**   95
**Index**   97
**Picture Credits**   103
**About the Author**   104

# FOREWORD

# "The Most Difficult Puzzles Ever Devised"

Charles Best, one of the pioneers in the search for a cure for diabetes, once explained what it is about medical research that intrigued him so. "It's not just the gratification of knowing one is helping people," he confided, "although that probably is a more heroic and selfless motivation. Those feelings may enter in, but truly, what I find best is the feeling of going toe to toe with nature, of trying to solve the most difficult puzzles ever devised. The answers are there somewhere, those keys that will solve the puzzle and make the patient well. But how will those keys be found?"

Since the dawn of civilization, nothing has so puzzled people—and often frightened them, as well—as the onset of illness in a body or mind that had seemed healthy before. A seizure, the inability of a heart to pump, the sudden deterioration of muscle tone in a small child—being unable to reverse such conditions or even to understand why they occur was unspeakably frustrating to healers. Even before there were names for

# Foreword

such conditions, even before they were understood at all, each was a reminder of how complex the human body was, and how vulnerable.

While our grappling with understanding diseases has been frustrating at times, it has also provided some of humankind's most heroic accomplishments. Alexander Fleming's accidental discovery in 1928 of a mold that could be turned into penicillin has resulted in the saving of untold millions of lives. The isolation of the enzyme insulin has reversed what was once a death sentence for anyone with diabetes. There have been great strides in combating conditions for which there is not yet a cure, too. Medicines can help AIDS patients live longer, diagnostic tools such as mammography and ultrasounds can help doctors find tumors while they are treatable, and laser surgery techniques have made the most intricate, minute operations routine.

This "toe-to-toe" competition with diseases and disorders is even more remarkable when seen in a historical continuum. An astonishing amount of progress has been made in a very short time. Just two hundred years ago, the existence of germs as a cause of some diseases was unknown. In fact, it was less than 150 years ago that a British surgeon named Joseph Lister had difficulty persuading his fellow doctors that washing their hands before delivering a baby might increase the chances of a healthy delivery (especially if they had just attended to a diseased patient)!

Each book in Lucent's Diseases and Disorders series explores a disease or disorder and the knowledge that has been accumulated (or discarded) by doctors through the years. Each book also examines the tools used for pinpointing a diagnosis, as well as the various means that are used to treat or cure a disease. Finally, new ideas are presented—techniques or medicines that may be on the horizon.

Frustration and disappointment are still part of medicine, for not every disease or condition can be cured or prevented. But the limitations of knowledge are being pushed outward constantly; the "most difficult puzzles ever devised" are finding challengers every day.

## INTRODUCTION

# Naming a Nightmare

There are almost as many types of cancer as there are parts of the human body. Some are more life-threatening than others. Despite this, anyone diagnosed with even the least threatening type of cancer usually experiences a great deal of stress and fear. When a physician tells a patient he or she has some type of cancer, both the patient and the patient's family know that they are about to undergo some drastic changes, even if the person afflicted has a type and stage of cancer with a very high survival rate. Even before the diagnosis is actually made, the wondering and waiting are hard on everyone.

Novelist Maureen McHugh shared some of her first thoughts as she awaited test results before she was diagnosed with Hodgkin's lymphoma (also known as Hodgkin's disease):

> Bob, my husband, was in Toronto. He had just gotten there. So I called him from the [medical center] parking lot. I said the doctor was concerned, and that it might be lymphoma. But they wouldn't know if it was lymphoma or an infection until they did a biopsy. I didn't want to tell him in Canada, away from home, but I wanted to tell someone . . . I think things like, maybe I won't outlive the dog—and I won't have to go through Smith's [the dog] death from old age . . . I will never be in a nursing home.[1]

# Naming a Nightmare

## A Brief History

Scores of people have dealt with similar anxious moments when facing a possible diagnosis of one of the many types of cancer that have been identified and studied in the last century. However, physicians and scientists have been aware of other types of cancer for much longer. Hodgkin's disease, for instance, was first described more than three hundred years ago. The symptoms of Hodgkin's disease, or Hodgkin's lymphoma, were first described

Pathologist Thomas Hodgkin was the first to describe the cancer of the lymphatic system, which would eventually bear his name, while on staff at Guy's Hospital in London, England, in 1832.

in 1666 by the Italian scientist and physician Marcello Malpighi in his paper "De Viscerum Structura Exercitatio Anatomica."

Although the condition was described hundreds of years earlier, it was not given the name it is known by today until 1865. Hodgkin's disease was named for Dr. Thomas Hodgkin. Hodgkin joined the staff of Guy's Hospital in London, England, in 1825, after graduating from Edinburgh Medical School, in Edinburgh, Scotland. While at Guy's Hospital, Hodgkin studied and cataloged tissue samples of abnormal spleens and lymph nodes. The results of his research, released in 1832, revealed a great deal of information about a medical condition that affects lymph nodes all over the body, although at that time it was not identified as a form of cancer. Despite his extensive study, though, he was not credited with the discovery of this condition for many years.

Hodgkin was overlooked in other ways, as well. Even though Hodgkin's research and knowledge were extensive, he was repeatedly passed over for a teaching position. He left Guy's in 1837, devoting the remainder of his career to the welfare of native people in colonial countries. He died in Palestine, what is today Israel, in 1866. A year before his death he finally was credited with his discovery. Hodgkin's recognition came about due to the work of two other physicians at Guy's, Dr. Richard Bright and Sir Samuel Wilks.

Bright was an expert on kidney disease. He wrote a paper about abdominal tumors, which included information about two of Hodgkin's cases. Then, in 1856, Sir Samuel Wilks, a pathologist at Guy's, described several postmortem (after someone has died) cases that had "a peculiar enlargement of the lymphatic glands frequently associated with disease of the spleen."[2] Wilks's report had touched on several of Hodgkin's original case studies, which had been preserved in the hospital's museum. During his study, Wilks also came across Bright's references to Hodgkin's original work, and so, ultimately, he gave Hodgkin the credit for the discovery.

One of Wilks's contributions to the study of Hodgkin's disease was his use of the microscope in examining affected tissue. In fact, the microscope was Wilks's primary tool for studying diseased lymph glands. By using the microscope, he was able to recognize large cells present in the lymph nodes and the spleen that are characteristic of Hodgkin's disease. Then, in 1878, Dr. W.S. Greenfield made the first drawings of Hodgkin's-involved lymph nodes, also by observing them under a low-power microscope.

In the late 1800s and early 1900s, Hodgkin's disease became a hot topic for argument among noted physicians and scientists of the day. Based on a number of case studies, Dr. Carl Sternberg and Dr. Dorothy Reed had provided extensive microscopic descriptions of the appearance of Hodgkin's-diseased cells, but they disagreed as to what actually caused it. Since over half of the subjects in Sternberg's case studies also had tuberculosis, he believed that Hodgkin's disease was closely connected with tuberculosis. Reed and others disagreed, however. She believed that Hodgkin's had no specific association with tuberculosis, other than the fact that some patients with Hodgkin's might also have tuberculosis. Reed believed that Hodgkin's was an inflammation of the lymph tissues, rather than a malignancy. Still other physicians believed that Hodgkin's was actually a cancer of the lymph nodes. As research continued in the early decades of the twentieth century, this proved to be true.

## Unsuccessful Early Treatments

With Hodgkin's disease identified as a type of cancer, physicians and scientists began to work on ways to try to treat it. Some of these treatments proved to be as dangerous as the disease itself. As far back as the 1800s, Hodgkin's was treated with substances such as arsenic and iodine, which sometimes made the patients even more ill than they already were. Later, in the early decades of the 1900s, physicians began battling Hodgkin's disease with two types of radiation treatments. One was the administration of small doses of radiation to the entire trunk of the body over a period of many weeks. In the other treatment, one large dose of radiation was applied directly to

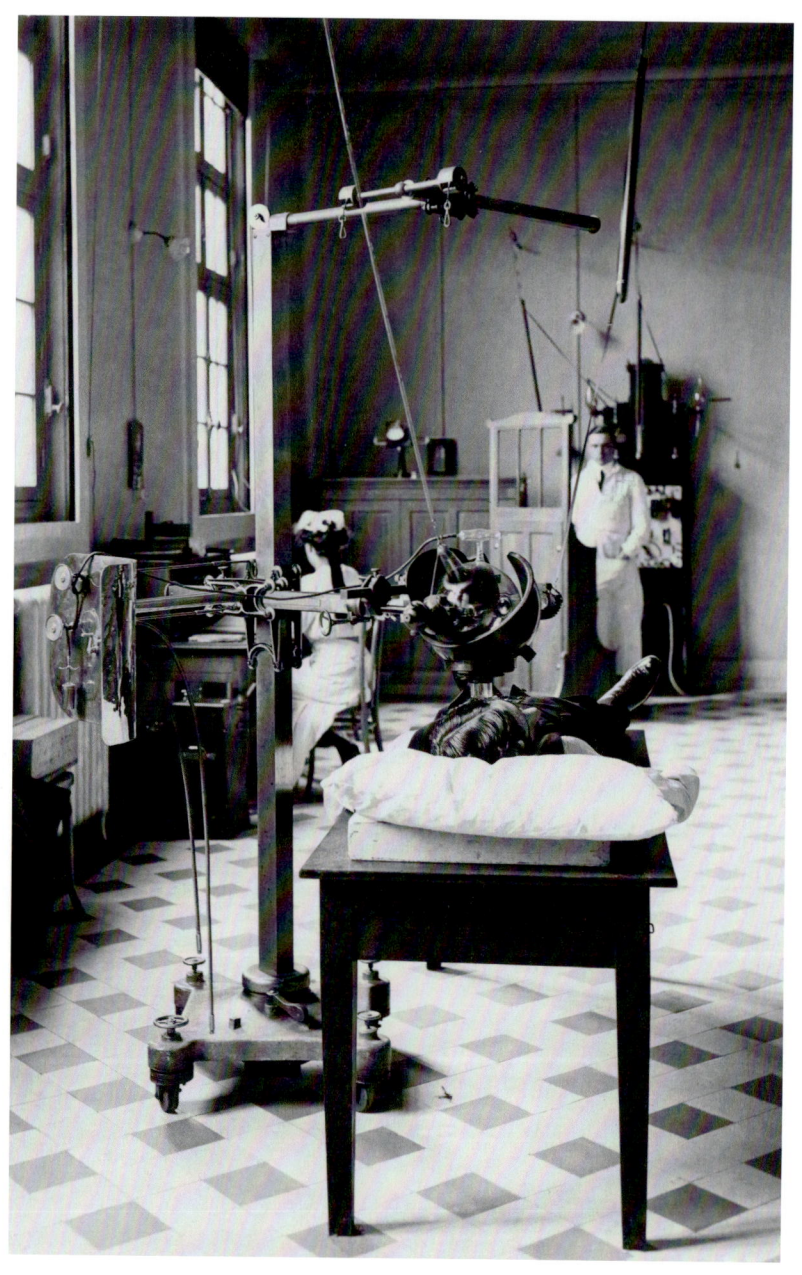

A patient receiving radiotherapy in the early 1900s. During the first part of the twentieth century some doctors believed that treating the whole body with radiation was the best way to cure Hodgkin's disease.

the tumor. However, results of both types of treatment were ultimately unsuccessful. The cancer returned and spread to previously healthy lymph nodes, and the disease became more resistant to radiation treatment. None of the patients who received these two types of radiation therapy survived. For the next four decades, most physicians restricted themselves to trying to make patients more comfortable, rather than trying to cure the disease. They focused on devising ways to shrink the enlarged nodes that interfered with breathing and other normal body functions. It was not until the 1940s that treatments were developed which actually boosted five- and ten-year survival rates to more than 80 percent, and this type of cancer was no longer a certain death sentence. Finally, Hodgkin's lymphoma patients had hope of waking from this particular nightmare.

CHAPTER ONE

# What is Hodgkin's Disease?

Hodgkin's disease is a type of lymphoma. Lymphoma describes the types of cancer that develop in the lymphatic system, which is a part of the body's immune system. A rare condition, Hodgkin's disease accounts for only about 1 percent of all diagnosed cancer cases in the United States, or about 7,400 new cases a year. Additionally, about twice as many cases are diagnosed in men than in women. Although Hodgkin's disease can occur in both adults and children, it is more common in two age groups; age fifteen to forty and after age fifty-five. This type of cancer is most rare in children under five years of age.

Hodgkin's lymphoma is not the only cancer associated with the lymphatic system, though. Hodgkin's is identified by the presence of a certain type of giant cells in the lymphatic tissue, most of which have more than one nucleus. These cells are called Reed-Sternberg cells. They were named for the physicians who first extensively studied and described them. Non-Hodgkin's lymphoma, however, is the name that applies to the other types of cancer that occur in the lymphatic system. There are about thirty different types of non-Hodgkin's lymphoma. These lymphoma do not contain the giant cells. In fact, non-Hodgkin's lymphoma is much more common than Hodgkin's disease.

## What is Hodgkin's Disease? 15

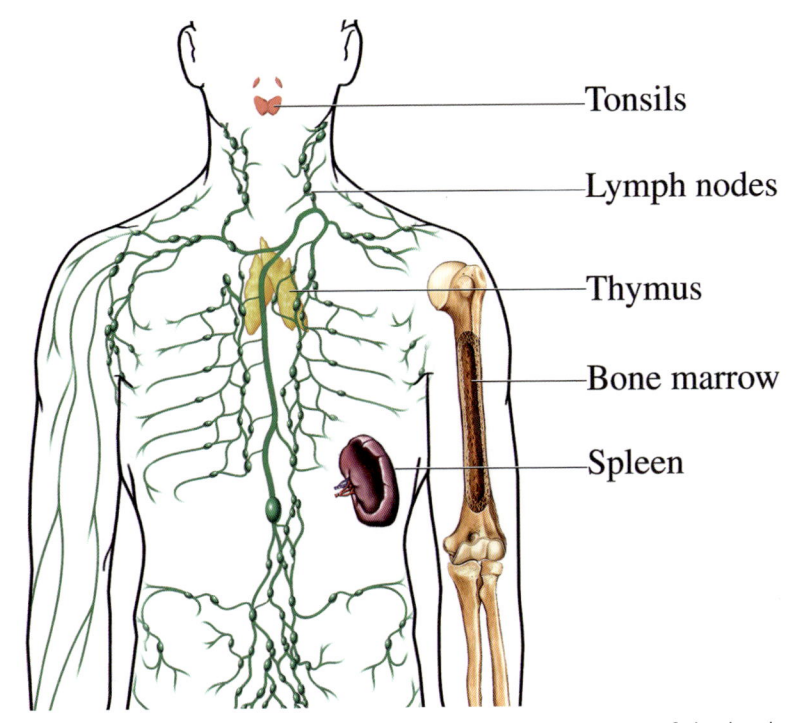

An illustration of the human lymphatic system, the part of the body where Hodgkin's disease develops.

    The lymphatic system operates similar to blood vessels, but instead of transporting blood, the lymphatic system transports a colorless, watery fluid called lymph throughout the body. Lymph contains cells called lymphocytes, which fight infection. Along this transportation network are grape-like clusters of small organs called lymph nodes. Lymph nodes are located in the underarms, chest, abdomen, neck, and groin. The spleen, thymus, tonsils, and bone marrow are also part of the lymphatic system. Lymphatic tissue is found in other parts of the body, as well, such as the intestines, skin, and stomach.

    As with other types of cancer, in Hodgkin's disease cells in the lymphatic system begin to grow and divide rapidly and randomly. Since lymphatic tissue is present in so many parts of the body, Hodgkin's disease can start almost anywhere. For instance, it can start in only one lymph node and progress to a group of lymph nodes, the spleen, or even bone marrow.

There is more than one type of Hodgkin's disease. In fact, once the medical team has determined which type of Hodgkin's lymphoma a person has, the condition can be further identified by stage. There are five distinct types of Hodgkin's and four progressive stages.

## Types of Hodgkin's Disease

The five subtypes of Hodgkin's lymphoma are nodular sclerosis, mixed cellularity, lymphocyte-depleted, nodular lymphocyte predominant Hodgkin's disease, and lymphocyte-rich classical Hodgkin's lymphoma. Though some of the names are quite lengthy, these names provide clues to how the different subtypes actually affect the body.

The most common type of Hodgkin's disease, nodular sclerosis, accounts for around 60 percent of all Hodgkin's cases. This type of Hodgkin's appears as nodules in lymph nodes in the lower neck, collar bone area, the center of the chest, and sometimes spreads to the lungs. It is characterized by a type of Reed-Sternberg cells called lacunar cells. In lacunar cells, the cytoplasm, the jelly-like substance between the cell wall and

A photomicrograph of a Reed-Sternberg cell surrounded by lymphocytes indicates that a patient has nodular sclerosis or mixed celluarity, two subtypes of Hodgkin's disease.

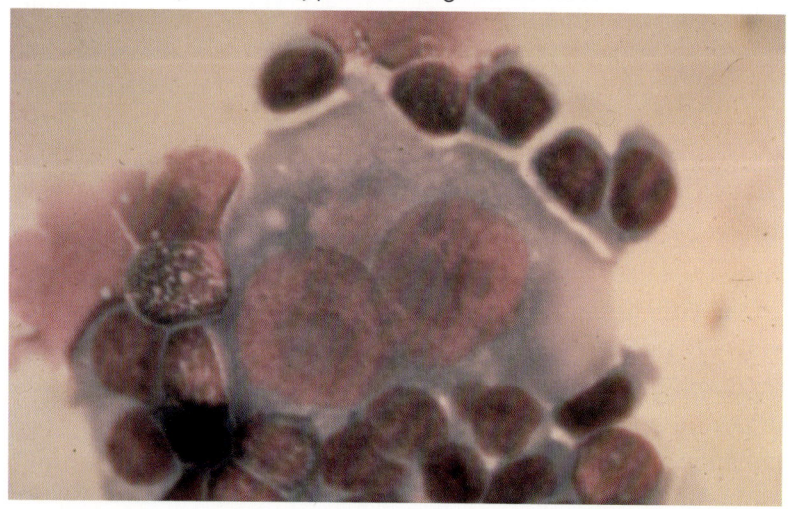

## What is Hodgkin's Disease?

the nucleus, shrinks, leaving an empty space around the nucleus of the cell. Apparently on the rise in recent years, nodular sclerosis is the type of Hodgkin's most frequently diagnosed in younger patients. Additionally, although the reason is not known, it is the one type of Hodgkin's diagnosed more frequently in women than in men. Many describe the previously mentioned symptoms, fever and night sweats, and sometimes body aches when they are questioned about recent health issues.

A forty-four-year-old patient described her medical condition prior to being diagnosed with nodular sclerosis, "I have had swollen glands in my neck with knots for one year. Each doctor's visit I was given another antibiotic. I developed bronchitis and pneumonia and the x-ray showed a mass."[3]

The second most common subtype is mixed cellularity, which accounts for about 20 to 30 percent of the patients currently being treated for Hodgkin's disease. Mixed cellularity most frequently affects older patients, children under ten years of age, and people with immune disorders, such as Acquired Immune Deficiency Disorder (AIDS). Among the adult group, and again for reasons unknown, more men tend to be affected than women.

When tissues are examined under magnification, Reed-Sternberg cells and inflammatory cells are very apparent in mixed cellularity Hodgkin's disease, which makes the diagnosis quite obvious. However, this subtype is often not diagnosed until it is in advanced stages. Despite this, though, a later diagnosis does not necessarily affect the outcome of the treatment.

The next type of Hodgkin's disease is called lymphocyte-depleted. Lymphocyte-depleted Hodgkin's accounts for about 4 to 5 percent of all patients diagnosed with some type of Hodgkin's disease. Usually, this type of Hodgkin's is diagnosed in elderly people. The cancer involvement with lymphocyte-depleted Hodgkin's disease is extensive, and the prognosis is poor. Without extensive testing, this condition can be confused with non-Hodgkin's lymphoma.

A fourth subtype of Hodgkin's, nodular lymphocyte predominance, accounts for about 5 percent of all cases of Hodgkin's. It affects more men than women, particularly young men, and frequently the young men have no physical symptoms of the disease.

This subtype is different from the other four in one major respect. Malignant cells found in this type of Hodgkin's lymphoma are different from the classic Reed-Sternberg cells normally associated with the disease. In fact, Reed-Sternberg cells are very rarely found in this subtype of Hodgkin's. The cells associated with lymphocyte-predominance are lymphocytic and histolytic cells, or L&H cells. They are sometimes referred to as popcorn cells, because they vaguely resemble popcorn.

Lymphocyte-predominance is a very slow-growing form of Hodgkin's disease. Because it is so slow-growing, there is generally a long survival rate. There is, however, another risk factor associated with this particular subtype of Hodgkin's disease. Lymphocyte-predominance has about a 3 percent risk of later transforming into non-Hodgkin's lymphoma.

The final subtype of Hodgkin's disease, lymphocyte-rich classical Hodgkin's lymphoma, is similar to nodular-lymphocyte predominance in that it has few of the Reed-Sternberg cells. However, its cellular characteristics are more like that of mixed cellularity, nodular sclerosis, and lymphocyte-depleted. It accounts for about 5 percent of all Hodgkin's cases and is one of the types of Hodgkin's disease that affect children.

To further understand the rarity of Hodgkin's lymphoma, the number of diagnosed cases can be broken down by percentages among the five subtypes. As previously mentioned, about 1 percent of all diagnosed cancer cases, or about 7,400 a year, are Hodgkin's disease. That means that about 4,800 of these cases are nodular sclerosis, the most common subtype. Around 1,850, a number comparable to the total number of students at a large high school, are diagnosed with mixed cellularity. Lymphocyte-rich classical Hodgkin's lymphoma, lymphocyte-depleted, and nodular lymphocyte predominant each account for about 370 cases. These numbers may appear large at first glance, but approximately 740,000 cases of different types of cancer are diagnosed every year. This number is equal to about twice the population of Houston, Texas. When

# What is Hodgkin's Disease?

the Hodgkin's disease cases are compared to that figure, the number of Hodgkin's disease diagnoses is actually quite small.

## Stages of Hodgkin's Disease

In addition to diagnosing Hodgkin's by subtype, the medical team can gather further information about the degree to which the condition has progressed. This is called staging. As with other types of cancer, Hodgkin's lymphoma is a very active disease. Undetected and untreated, Hodgkin's disease can be expected to advance through four progressive stages. The stage at which it is identified helps determine the course of treatment. Once Hodgkin's disease is diagnosed, the medical team is able to use the identifiable characteristics of the stages and other information related to the staging to help them determine how far the disease has spread. This information is important in helping the medical team decide which procedures will be most effective in treating the patient. The staging process is also important because, although there can be exceptions, the progression of Hodgkin's disease is usually fairly predictable. It generally

The most common symptom of Hodgkin's disease is swollen glands, although having swollen glands does not always mean a person has Hodgkin's disease.

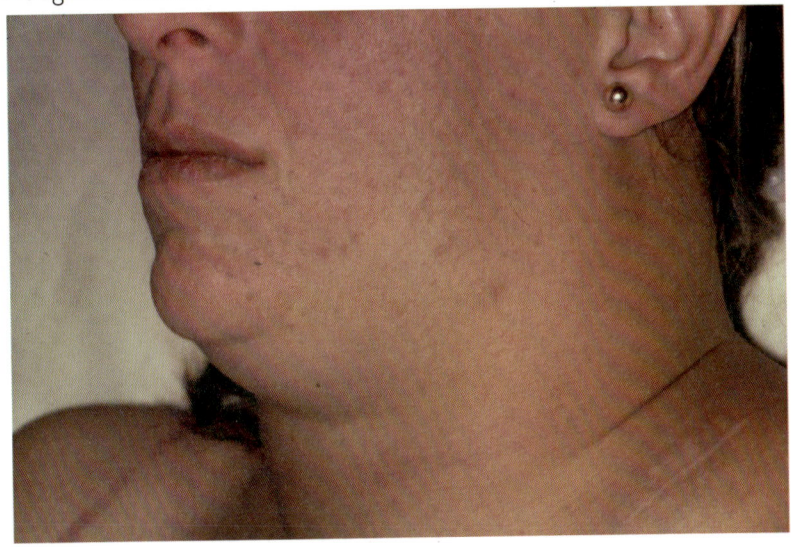

starts in only one set of lymph nodes, and then spreads to other lymph nodes and lymphatic tissue nearby. It does not usually skip around in the body until the disease is far advanced.

Stage I is the earliest stage, and Stage IV the most advanced. However, this does not mean that people in Stage IV cannot expect favorable results from their treatment. In fact, treatment of many Stage IV cases of Hodgkin's lymphoma has been successful. Therefore, the stage to which Hodgkin's disease has progressed does not necessarily predict how well the patient will respond to treatment.

In Stage I, Hodgkin's disease is usually found only in one lymph node area, or has progressed only to the tissue adjacent to that lymph node. In Stage II, Hodgkin's is in two or more lymph node areas on the same side of the diaphragm and may extend to nearby tissue. Patients are usually at Stage II when they are diagnosed with nodular sclerosis. Stage III means that Hodgkin's has progressed to lymph node areas on both sides of the diaphragm and may have extended to an adjacent organ or possibly to the spleen. Stage IV can be identified in two ways. Either the cancer has been detected in one or more organs outside the lymphatic system, or the cancer has spread outside the lymphatic system, and other lymph nodes are involved, as well.

Hodgkin's patients need to be aware that Hodgkin's disease might continue to advance during treatment or may return after treatment. Although there has been great success in the treatment of Hodgkin's disease, there is no such thing as 100 percent certainty that the disease will never come back. That is why patients continue to be monitored for the presence or progression of Hodgkin's disease both during and after treatment.

The stages are additionally broken down into "A" or "B." "A" is asymptomatic, which means these patients may not experience any of the symptoms associated with Hodgkin's disease. "B" patients, however, do experience some symptoms of the disease.

At first, some of the symptoms, such as fever and chills, fatigue, and night sweats, might be mistaken for influenza or anemia. Other symptoms include unexplained weight loss, loss of appetite, shortness of breath, bruising or easy bleeding, recurring

# A Successful Partnership

Much of today's success in treating Hodgkin's disease can be credited to Dr. Henry S. Kaplan and Dr. Saul Rosenberg. Together, they designed a linear accelerator for treating cancer. They spent the 1960s and 1970s doing extensive clinical research on Hodgkin's disease. Before their research, the main goal of Hodgkin's treatment was a palliative approach, to keep the patient as comfortable as possible for as long as possible. Because of their work, many of today's treatments for Hodgkin's disease have a success rate of 90 percent or higher.

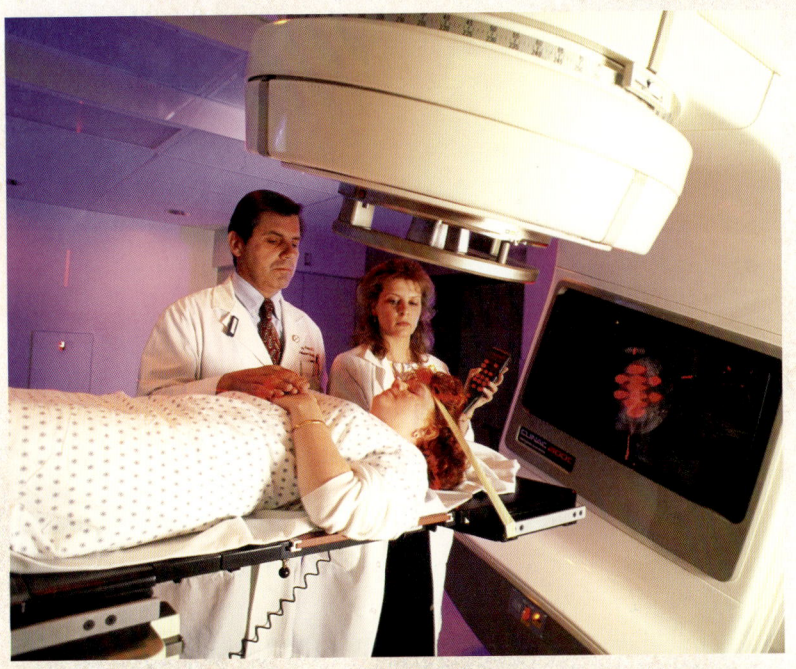

Doctors preparing a patient for treatment with a linear accelerator. This machine, designed by Henry S. Kaplan and Saul Rosenberg, has been extremely successful in treating Hodgkin's disease.

infections, bone, nerve, or abdominal pain, and severe itching for no apparent reason. The presence of any of these symptoms does not necessarily mean a person has Hodgkin's disease, though. The most telling symptom is swelling of the lymph nodes, especially those in the neck, armpits, or groin. However, even swollen glands are not a sure indication of Hodgkin's disease. An accurate diagnosis of Hodgkin's disease, or any other medical condition, requires extensive testing by a team of medical experts, specifically trained to know how to identify these conditions.

## Successful Outcomes

As continuing research yields more advanced treatment programs, more patients are experiencing longer periods of

# Kids with Cancer

Children with Hodgkin's disease and other types of cancer have special needs. First, they may experience side effects from treatments years later, when they are adults. These potential problems include infertility, heart or blood pressure problems, learning disabilities, dental problems, and the risk of developing other types of cancer in later years.

Children may also suffer from emotional side effects due to pain, separation from their families and normal routines, and the fear of death. This can be especially difficult for young children who cannot understand what is happening to them. Because of this, many hospitals have behavioral medicine departments that help children cope with these issues. Many hospitals provide home-like settings, like Ronald McDonald House, for children and their parents, and Kim's Place, a hangout for teens and young adults established at M.D. Anderson Hospital in Houston, Texas, by Houston Comets basketball star Kim Perrot, who later lost her own battle with lung cancer. These settings provide normalcy and emotional relief for young cancer patients and their families.

# What is Hodgkin's Disease?

remission and others become symptom free. Survival rates are measured during a five-year period. These rates show the percentage of patients who continue to live at least five years after Hodgkin's disease is diagnosed and treated. Five years should not be considered a limit, however. Many people live much longer than five years after they are treated and remain cancer-free, and according to the most recent statistics available, many people currently being treated for Hodgkin's disease can expect a favorable outcome. Hodgkin's disease patients diagnosed and treated while still in Stage I or Stage II have a five-year survival rate of 90 to 95 percent. In Stage III, the five-year survival rate is 85 to 90 percent. Stage IV Hodgkin's, while the most advanced stage, still has a high five-year survival rate of about 80 to 85 percent. These statistics are encouraging to both patients and their families as they go through the treatment process, and even as high as survival rates currently are, researchers continue to work to boost them yet higher.

## Comparing Adult and Childhood Hodgkin's Disease

Despite its rarity and favorable survival rate, the diagnosis of Hodgkin's disease or any other type of cancer is a frightening and stressful event. It is even more so for parents whose children have been diagnosed with the disease. They are in the position of trying to deal with their personal feelings, comforting and reassuring their children (some of whom are too young to understand what is happening to them), and educating themselves for the trying times ahead.

As previously stated, the two types of Hodgkin's disease that affect children are classical Hodgkin's lymphoma and nodular lymphocyte predominant Hodgkin's lymphoma. Physical symptoms are the same as those of adults with Hodgkin's: painful, swollen lymph nodes in the chest, neck, underarm, or groin area; fever; night sweats; itchy skin; and weight loss for no apparent reason. Also the same as in adult patients, the child's chances of recovery depend on the stage at which the

Hodgkin's is diagnosed, the size of the tumor and how well it responds to initial treatment, whether a brother or a sister has had Hodgkin's lymphoma, and whether the child has had the condition previously. However, the trait that applies only to children is the age group. Hodgkin's lymphoma generally occurs in young people between the ages of five and the middle teen years, roughly kindergarten to ninth grade.

Even if a child is successfully treated and in remission or pronounced cured of an episode of Hodgkin's disease, there are factors connected with Hodgkin's that can affect this child when he or she becomes an adult. First, as in adults, there is a possibility of recurrence of Hodgkin's or the development of another type of cancer in adult survivors of childhood Hodgkin's. Depending on the study, the risk rate is somewhere between 10 and 12 percent.

According to Rand El-Zein, MD, PhD, of M.D. Anderson Hospital in Houston, Texas, "It is particularly devastating for young adults to be hit with Hodgkin's disease, do well, and then face another cancer ten to 20 years down the line . . ."[4]

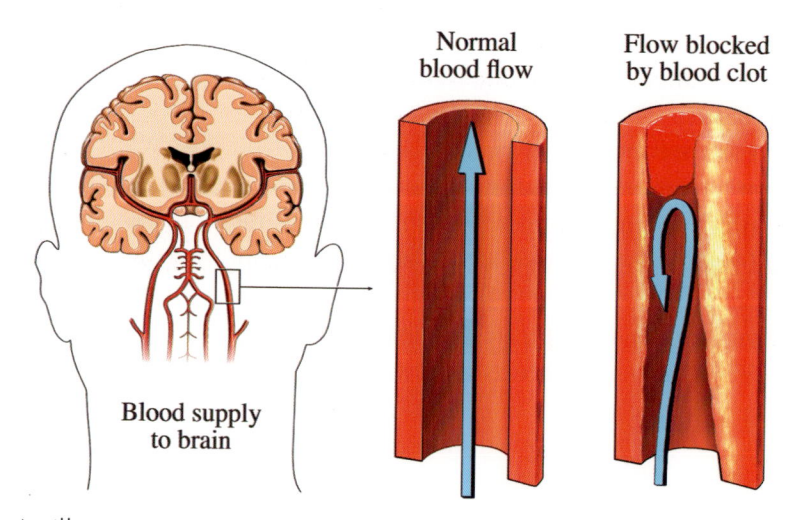

An illustration comparing the normal blood flow to the brain and when the flow is block by a blood clot such as when a person experiences a stroke. Many adult survivors of childhood Hodgkin's disease run the slight risk of having a stroke in later years.

Secondly, some adult survivors of childhood Hodgkin's disease who were treated with intensive chemotherapy experience symptoms of extreme depression and some suffer from somatic distress. This means physical symptoms such as dizziness, faintness, and upset stomach during stressful situations. Although childhood Hodgkin's occurs more frequently in boys than in girls, these episodes of depression and somatic distress occur more frequently in female adult survivors than in males. It is believed that women tend to suffer more from such psychiatric issues because women tend to worry more than men. Additionally, survivors of childhood Hodgkin's run the risk of not being able to have children. A final threat to these adult survivors is a slight risk of stroke. A stroke occurs when a blood clot blocks an artery or a blood vessel breaks, interrupting the flow of blood to the brain. When this happens, brain cells die, resulting in brain damage. Studies are presently being conducted to determine specifically if high-dose radiation in young Hodgkin's patients might increase their risk of suffering strokes as adults. Other issues factored into these studies include a history of smoking, high blood pressure, or diabetes. These studies are still ongoing.

All in all, both adults and children who have been treated for any type of Hodgkin's disease may face future health risks and should monitor their health with regular checkups. It is also vitally important that adult patients and parents of young Hodgkin's disease patients educate themselves regarding symptoms and treatments so they can request medical attention if they think they need it. The sooner a problem is suspected and diagnosed, the greater the chances of a favorable outcome.

CHAPTER TWO

# Diagnosing Hodgkin's Disease

From the time a person first suspects a serious medical problem such as Hodgkin's disease, many people say that the hardest part of the diagnosis is waiting for the results of the various tests. These results frequently are not ready for the medical team's interpretation for a few days to a week or more. During these anxious days, sometimes it helps to talk with close friends or relatives or to contact a support group.

Since there are several different types of Hodgkin's disease and the disease progresses through different stages, usually a single treatment program is not appropriate for each type or stage of the condition. Correctly identifying the subtype of Hodgkin's a person has and the stage to which the condition has progressed is vitally important in planning appropriate treatment. A thorough physical examination, an extensive interview process, and a variety of testing procedures are used by the medical team to correctly identify a patient's subtype of Hodgkin's lymphoma. The testing procedure can range from something as totally painless as X-rays, to procedures that may be frightening and uncomfortable, like biopsies and exploratory surgery. These testing procedures are necessary, however, and should be viewed as first steps on the road to recovery.

While awaiting test results, it is important to remember that symptoms such as swollen glands can occur for a variety of

# Diagnosing Hodgkin's Disease

reasons that have nothing to do with cancer, and sometimes the swelling can go away on its own. During the diagnostics process, the patient and the patient's family need to stick as close to a normal routine as possible. This gives people a sense of control over their lives even when it seems that their health might be temporarily out of their control.

## Physical Examinations and Medical History

Sometimes, the first person who suspects the possibility of Hodgkin's lymphoma is the person who is actually affected. As Karen Gessner, a licensed cancer social worker at OSF Saint Anthony Medical Center in Rockford, Illinois, who deals with

Just like any ordinary check up, Hodgkin's patients must be given a complete physical examination, so the medical team can determine the best course of treatment.

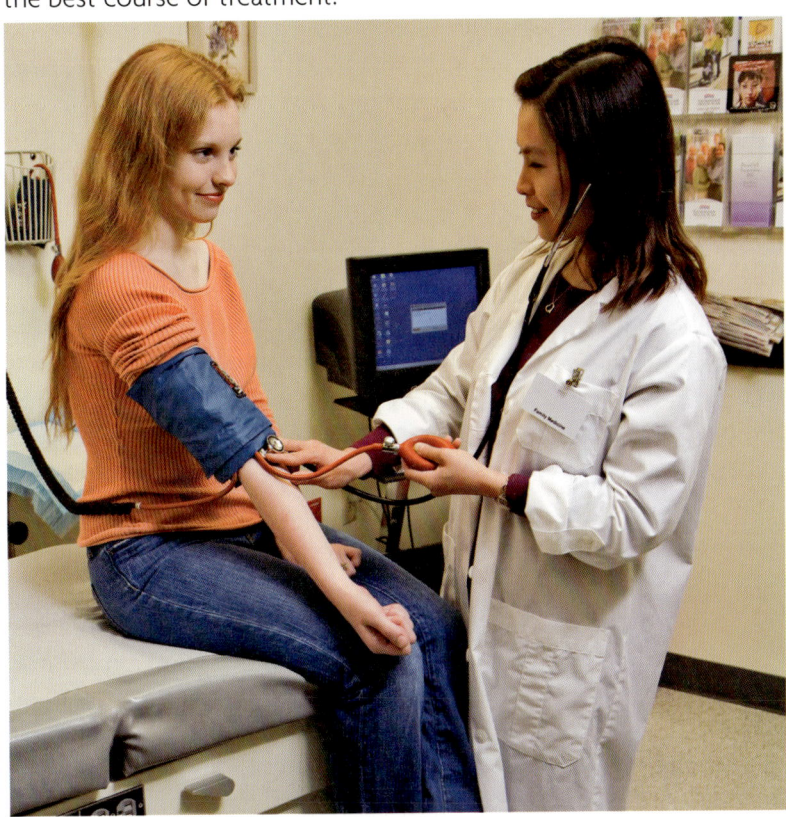

these diagnoses on a daily basis described, "Most often when a patient comes in for a diagnosis, he or she has a strong feeling about what might be wrong. If it is an adult, he or she almost always brings a family member for support."[5]

This individual may have felt swollen lymph nodes, noticed an uncharacteristic lack of energy, lower back pain, or any of the other symptoms of Hodgkin's lymphoma. At other times, though, the condition is detected during routine physical exams, such as yearly checkups or pregnancy exams. Regardless of how it is diagnosed, learning that a person has Hodgkin's or any other kind of cancer comes as a shock to the person diagnosed and to the individual's friends and family.

During the diagnostic process, physicians or their assistants will ask the patient questions about general health and family medical history. The medical team needs to know if anyone else in the family, such as parents, grandparents, aunts, uncles, or siblings has had Hodgkin's or any other type of cancer or serious medical condition. The medical team will ask about specific symptoms. This is not the time to try to make light of or explain away any symptoms. The patient should answer these questions as thoroughly and completely as possible and ask close family members if they can recall any additional information. The diagnosis or suspicion of Hodgkin's disease or any other type of cancer is a very stressful event in the patient's life, and this person may not recall bits of information, such as family history or other things that could be useful in diagnosis and treatment.

The patient or patient's family usually has questions, as well. Patients may want to know what tests will be conducted and what the tests will show. They may want to know if the tests will require a hospital stay, and if so, for how long, because schools or employers would need to be notified. They may want to know if any of the tests are painful, if there are any medical risks from taking the tests, and if any side effects could result from the tests. These are all reasonable questions, and the medical team would have no objections to answering these and any other questions the patient or the patient's family might have.

# Diagnosing Hodgkin's Disease

In addition to answering questions, the patient will be given a complete physical examination, much like any routine annual checkup. This would include pulse, temperature, and blood pressure, listening to the heart and lungs with a stethoscope, and physically feeling for swollen glands. If swelling is detected in the area of lymph glands, the physician might prescribe a course of antibiotics and have the patient return in a few weeks to see if the swelling has gone down or disappeared. Infections and other conditions that have nothing to do with Hodgkin's disease are often the cause of swollen glands.

At some point during the physical examination, the medical team will usually run a number of blood tests. Since blood flows throughout the body, blood tests are good indicators of general health. With just one stick of the needle, medical teams can run more than a dozen different diagnostic tests on the blood. These tests show if the red and white blood cells are in balance. Excessive white cells are one indicator of the presence of infection in the blood. Blood tests also indicate how well the kidneys and liver are functioning. Additionally, certain types of blood tests are good indicators of how a patient might respond to certain kinds of treatment. These tests reveal such information as the serum albumin level, which has to do with the liquid part of the blood and its ability to carry nutrients throughout the body. Other blood tests include the erythrocyte sedimentation rate, or ESR, which measures inflammation in the body, and a test for the presence of LDH, lactic dehydrogenase, in the blood, which can help indicate cell damage. Additionally, LDH levels are monitored to see how well Hodgkin's patients are responding to chemotherapy.

## X-Rays, CTs, MRIs, PETs, and Other Imaging Devices

Questionnaires, physical examinations, and blood work are only the beginning of the diagnostic process. Next comes a round of tests that to the patient might seem like a jumble of the alphabet. Once their functions are explained, though, they are not nearly so confusing. Something else patients often appreciate about these procedures is that except for the fact that some of these tests are performed after dyes are put into the body through an intravenous injection, called an IV, these tests are essentially noninvasive. This means surgery is not involved.

The X-ray is probably the diagnostic tool most familiar to patients. An X-ray is a stream of photons, particles carrying electromagnetic force, which can visually penetrate the body's surface, producing images of the body's internal structure, such as organs. For instance, the enlarged lymph nodes in the chest area caused by Hodgkin's disease can usually be seen on a plain chest X-ray.

Another way the medical team may take a look at lymph nodes in the chest and abdomen is with computed tomography, or CT. A CT scan creates pictures like an X-ray, but instead of taking one picture, the CT scan produces detailed

A magnetic resonance tomography, or MRI, is just one of the diagnostic tools that physicians might use to determine if a patient has Hodgkin's disease.

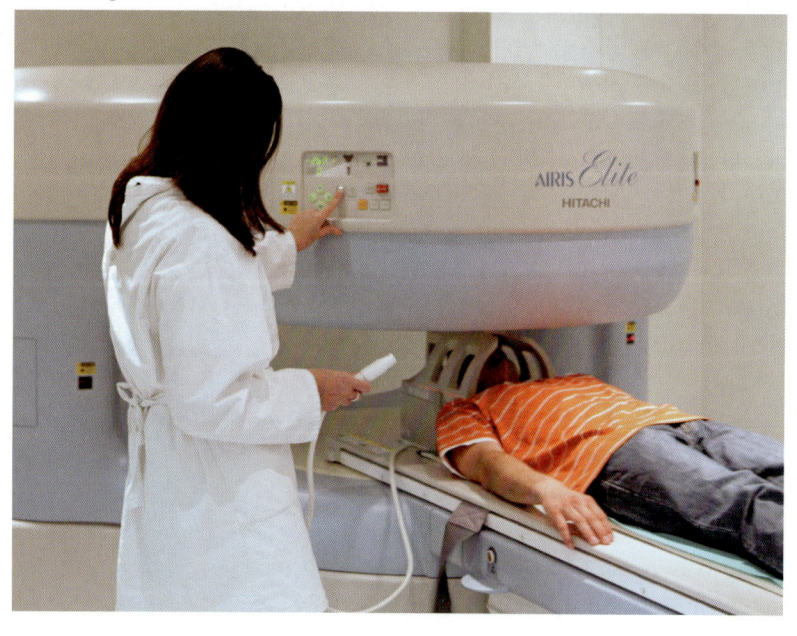

## Diagnosing Hodgkin's Disease

cross-sectional images of the body. The scanner takes many pictures as it rotates around the patient. These pictures are like visual slices of a loaf of bread, as the machine creates multiple images of the part of the body being studied.

Frequently, after the first set of pictures is taken, an intravenous dye, called a radiocontrast or contrasting agent, is injected into the body. A technician puts a tiny tube into the patient's arm, which causes little if any pain. The dye is then injected through this tube. This dye helps create a visual outline of the structures in the body. After the dye is injected, a second set of pictures is taken. Sometimes people feel flushed as the dye enters the body through the IV. Rarely, some people have more serious reactions, like hives, lowered blood pressure, or trouble breathing. The medical team needs to know if the patient has ever had a reaction to injected dyes. If so, the patient may need to drink a special contrast material before the second set of pictures is taken.

Another test the medical team may want to use to help make its diagnosis is magnetic resonance imaging, or MRI. The MRI is not used as frequently as other diagnostic devices, but physicians may want to use this device if there is any concern about a patient's spinal cord or brain. MRI scans use powerful magnets that release energy when turned on and off. This energy creates images that a computer then translates into pictures of the body part. The computer can use this information to create cross-sectional images of the body part, much like a CT scanner. When the machine is running, it produces a humming sound that can be mildly annoying. Some treatment centers provide the patient with headphones. The headphones produce music, blocking out the humming sound.

Sometimes the medical team uses radioactive substances to detect the presence of Hodgkin's disease. One radioactive test is the gallium scan. Gallium-67 is a radioactive substance that is injected into the body intravenously. Since it takes the body a couple of hours to absorb this substance into the areas where Hodgkin's is present or suspected, the patient is placed under a scanner to record radioactivity on film about two hours after the injection. This test usually produces no side effects.

A newer radioactive scanning device is called positron emission tomography, or PET. With a PET scan, the patient is given glucose, which is a form of sugar. This glucose contains a radioactive atom. The PET has a special camera that detects radioactivity. Cells with Hodgkin's disease absorb high amounts of the radioactive sugar, so the PET is able to pick up evidence of the presence of Hodgkin's disease very clearly.

Another type of imaging test is the lymphangiogram, which is an X-ray procedure using a radio opaque substance, a contrast medium. This test is used to look at lymph nodes in the pelvis and the abdomen and requires an injected blue dye. The dye is injected under the skin between the toes. From there, it travels through the lymphatic system to the nodes in the pelvis and the abdomen. The physician also injects a small amount of another contrast material, which will appear white on X-rays. The contrast between the colors helps the doctor detect enlarged lymph nodes that might be affected by Hodgkin's.

## Contrast Materials

The purpose of contrast materials, or contrast agents, is to improve the clarity of magnetic resonance images. The agents usually enter the body by being swallowed or injected. They increase the brightness in areas of the body by altering the nuclei of hydrogen cells. Although a number of contrast agents have been in use for over a decade, their effectiveness has been greatly improved in recent years. New contrast agents work longer in the body. This makes it possible to extend the imaging procedure without the patient having to swallow the agents again or be injected a second time.

## Diagnosing Hodgkin's Disease

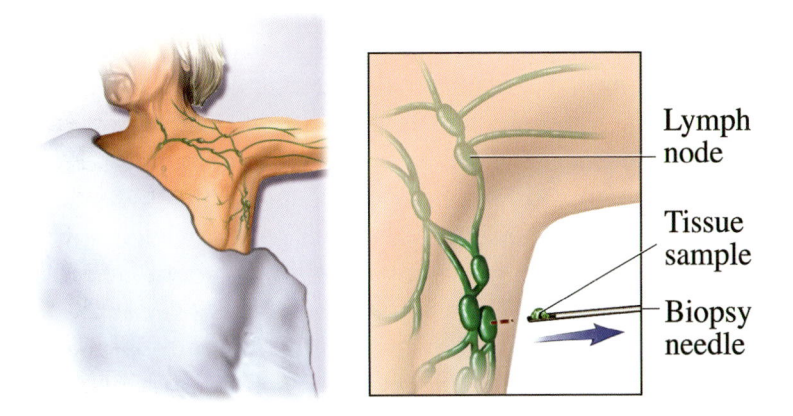

An illustration of a needle biopsy, a procedure where tissue is taken from a patient's lymph nodes to determine if Hodgkin's disease is present.

However, this test is not used as frequently as the PET and CT scans.

## Biopsies

Often, even the word biopsy makes people feel squeamish, and while biopsies can be uncomfortable they are an important part of the diagnostic process. Basically, a biopsy is performed by removing small samples of living tissue from any part of the body by means of a hollow needle or tube. These tissue samples are then examined under a microscope by a scientist called a pathologist. If the medical team suspects Hodgkin's disease, these tissue samples are taken from enlarged lymph node areas. Although the tissues are run through additional tests, in the case of suspected Hodgkin's the pathologist is mainly looking for evidence of the Reed-Sternberg cells, which are present in most types of Hodgkin's disease.

There are several types of biopsy procedures available, and the best one will be selected to fit the patient's particular needs. The first is for tissue samples both near the body's surface and deeper within the body. It is called fine needle aspiration, or FNA. In this test, a very fine hollow needle is attached to a syringe. The needle is then inserted into the swollen tissue mass. It is moved around a bit to break loose some of the cells. The cells are drawn up into the syringe and are placed on a glass slide for examination under a microscope. If there are suspicious lymph nodes deeper in the body, this thin needle can be guided into the nodes as it is viewed on a CT scan. FNA is useful in distinguishing between noncancerous conditions, like infections, and other types of cancer. These sample sizes are small, however, and sometimes larger tissue samples are needed.

Large needle, or core biopsy, uses larger needles to obtain tissue samples. Like FNA, core biopsy extractors can be guided through deep tissues by a CT scan. This type of biopsy is useful for patients who are not strong enough to tolerate invasive surgical procedures, such as surgical biopsies and exploratory surgery.

Bone marrow tissue can also be biopsied. Bone marrow biopsies can provide information about the blood and the lymphatic system. Usually, the biopsy is taken from the upper part of the hip or the breastbone. The patient is given a local anesthetic, which affects only the area of the mass, then a strong needle is guided through the skin and outer surface of the bone until it reaches the soft center part of the bone, called marrow. A syringe sucks out a small sample of the bone marrow, and as with other types of biopsies the tissue is examined under a microscope by a pathologist.

The final type of biopsy is the surgical biopsy. As its name implies, it is the most invasive of all the biopsy procedures. There are two ways surgical biopsies can be performed, incisional, which means cutting into tissue, and excisional, or cutting away tissue. If a small amount of tissue is removed, this is an incisional biopsy. If, however, a tumor mass is small enough to be completely removed by the biopsy procedure, this is called excisional biopsy. If the mass is near the surface of the skin, the surgeon will give the patient a local anesthetic to perform this procedure and the patient will probably remain

## Passing the Time After Surgery

Some Hodgkin's patients require exploratory surgery. Usually, the first step after surgery is the recovery room. In the recovery room, the patient's pulse, blood pressure, and breathing will be monitored until the anesthesia is out of his or her system. From there, the patient is moved to a room. The patient will be in the room for a day or more, depending on the extent of the surgery and the patient's overall health. This is a time for rest and recovery. Some books or magazines, or maybe a computer game, will help pass the time and keep the patient's mind occupied. For small children, drawing paper and crayons are handy to have.

A physical therapist may help the patient with light exercise. These exercises are important in keeping the lungs clear, the blood flowing, and retaining strength and mobility. Even if some of these exercises are a little uncomfortable, they will help speed the recovery time.

The best recovery tool a person can have at this time, though, is patience. It is important to follow the directions of the medical team as closely as possible and wait until they feel the patient is ready to go home. Following the medical team's guidelines will prevent relapses and shorten recovery time.

awake. If, however, the lymph node is deeper, such as in the chest or abdomen, the surgeon will give the patient a general anesthetic, which puts the patient completely to sleep for the entire procedure.

The discomfort of biopsy procedures varies. Some patients have very little pain, while others may experience discomfort for a day or so. For the patient's welfare, the physician may prescribe pain relievers and sedative medications to minimize discomfort and anxiety. Some clinics even use hypnosis, although this has not become common practice. Some products

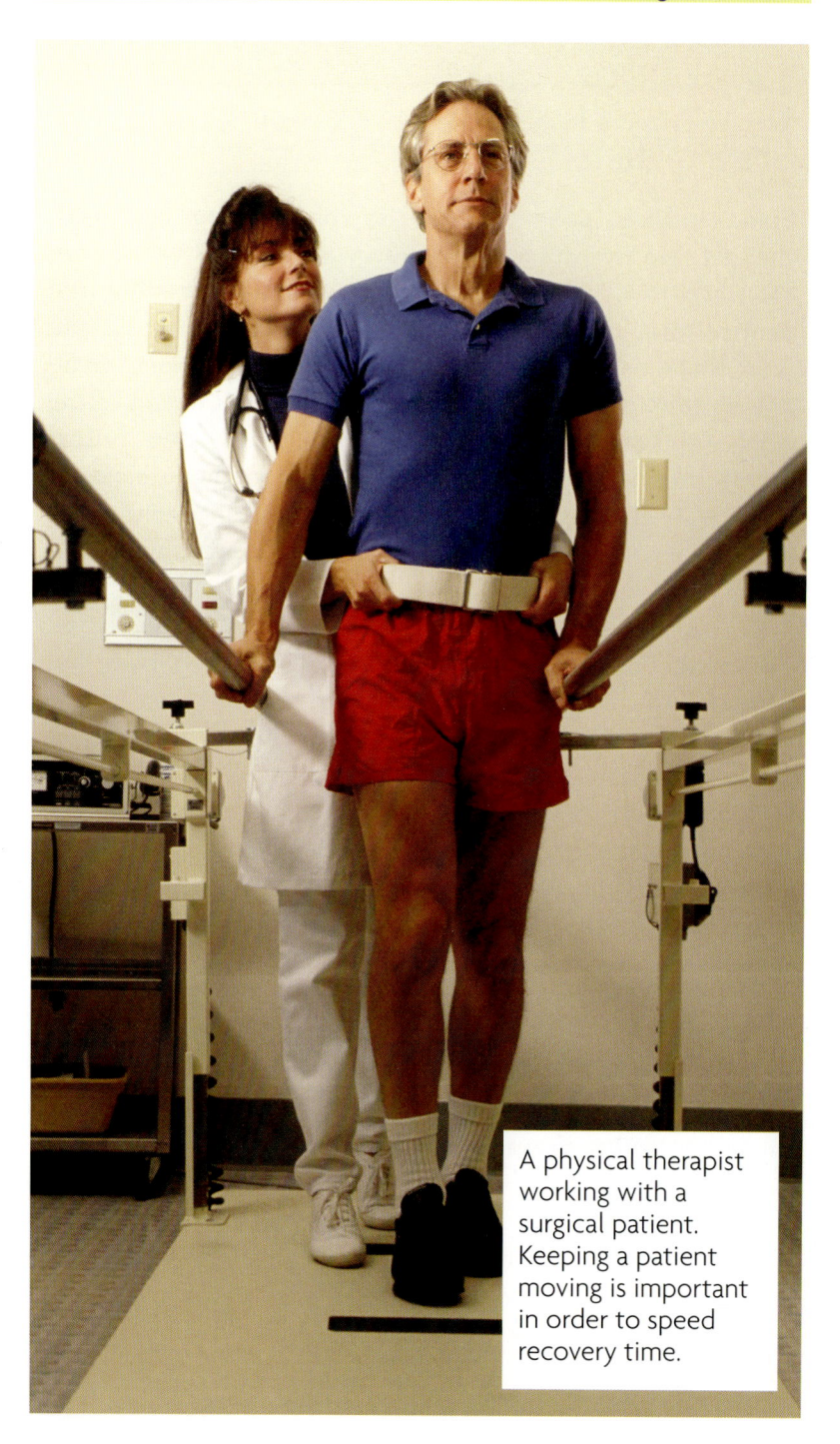

A physical therapist working with a surgical patient. Keeping a patient moving is important in order to speed recovery time.

# Diagnosing Hodgkin's Disease

have been developed, though, such as EMLA Cream, which dull skin pain during these procedures.

## Exploratory Surgery

There are those cases, however, for which a correct diagnosis requires more extensive procedures, such as exploratory surgeries. Though not used as extensively now as in the past, due to the invention of a wide range of imaging devices, surgical procedures are still the correct path to follow under certain conditions. Today, surgical procedures are primarily used to remove infected lymph nodes from the abdomen and to determine the extent to which the Hodgkin's disease has progressed.

Among these procedures are laparotomy and splenectomy. Although not performed as often now because of all of the imaging tests currently available, staging laparotomy is still sometimes offered to those patients in early stages of Hodgkin's

A computer graphic of a human spleen, a part of the body that works with the immune system. If Hodgkin's disease has spread to a patient's spleen, it can be removed by a procedure known as a splenectomy.

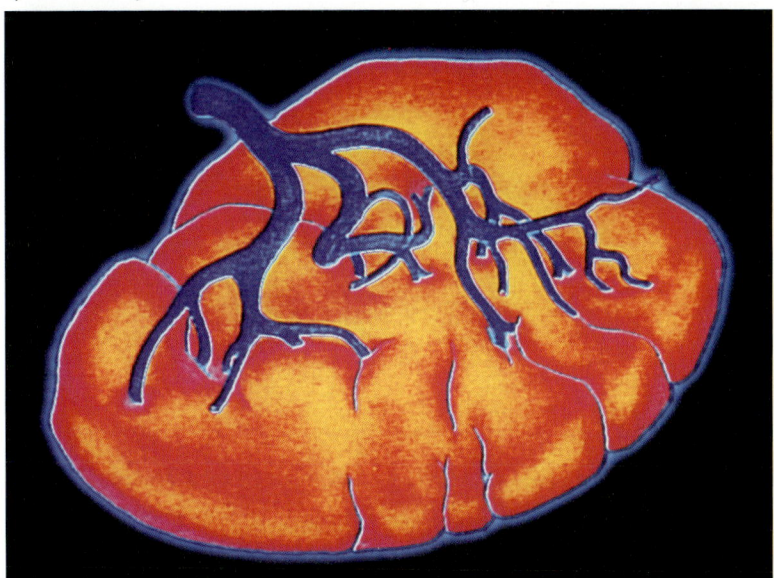

disease who have a good prognosis. This exploratory procedure can provide the patient with the assurance that the disease is not widespread, and the patient can avoid the risks associated with more extensive treatment.

The spleen is a lymphatic organ located to the left of the stomach, beneath the diaphragm. It works with the immune system, filtering foreign substances from the blood. It also acts as a reservoir, storing blood and destroying old blood cells. Despite its importance, however, the body can survive without the spleen, and if Hodgkin's has progressed to the spleen, that organ can be removed for the patient's welfare.

In fact, the results of one extensive study indicated that roughly one-half of the study's Hodgkin's patients had evidence of the disease in their spleens. However, in 25 percent of these cases, the spleen appeared outwardly normal. Only by removing and examining the spleen did the surgeons find evidence of Hodgkin's.

Although these are exploratory or diagnostic procedures, they are, nevertheless, invasive and traumatic to the body. Recovery time for these types of surgery varies according to the patient's overall health. The patient may expect a hospital stay of two to four days, and a period of four to six weeks for complete healing.

# CHAPTER THREE

# Treatments

Once a person receives the diagnosis of Hodgkin's disease, the patient and the medical team can begin making plans to move toward recovery. Physicians do not merely dictate to patients what treatments they will have. The patient has an active role in the treatment process. Each step in the treatment program will be carefully explained. Together, the patient and the medical team will decide on a treatment program best suited to the individual patient; one that will provide the patient with the best possible chances for recovery.

Treatment programs provide a number of options. In some instances, the medical team will focus on one specific course of treatment. In other cases, though, the medical team may put together a recovery program that involves more than one type of treatment. Whether a single type of treatment has been selected or more than one treatment will be used, these procedures will require several visits to a hospital or clinic and the medical team will probably recommend that someone accompany the patient to these appointments. The two types of treatments most often used in Hodgkin's disease are radiation therapy and chemotherapy.

## Chemotherapy

Chemotherapy is a type of cancer treatment that uses drugs to kill cancer cells. The first type of chemotherapy to be developed, and the type that is still most prevalent today, is called cytotoxic chemotherapy. An early drug used in cytotoxic

A patient receiving chemotherapy through intravenous injection, or IV. Although chemotherapy can be given orally, most Hodgkin's patients need to receive the treatment through IV.

# Treatments

therapy, called nitrogen mustard, was a form of a deadly chemical weapon that had been used in World War I. It is known as mustard gas. Scientists discovered that, although nitrogen mustard could cause some types of cancer, it could also be used to kill cancer cells. Nitrogen was first used on patients with lymphoma in 1942. It was injected in liquid form.

However, in its earliest days, chemotherapy was often as harmful to the patient as the disease. This is because doctors had to learn how much of these chemicals the patient could safely tolerate. They had to find a balance, a dosage that would attack the cancer cells without risking the patient's life. When doctors first started using chemotherapy to treat Hodgkin's disease and other forms of cancer, it was only given to people in advanced stages, people who had little to lose by risking this type of treatment. During the 1970s and 1980s, doctors were able to determine safe limits of these toxic drugs and began using them in earlier stages of cancer. Today, chemotherapy is a widely used and successful treatment for Hodgkin's lymphoma.

Cytoxic chemotherapy works by traveling to any part of the body where cancer cells are growing. They attack and damage the abnormal cells, so they are unable to divide and grow. As its name implies, the chemicals used in this type of chemotherapy are toxic, or poisonous. Because of this, doctors carefully regulate the dosage of these drugs when they are administered.

In most television programs and motion pictures actors playing chemotherapy patients are usually shown receiving the chemotherapy through an IV. Actually, though, chemotherapy drugs can be given in several ways: by IV, or intravenous injection with the drugs entering the body through a tube attached to a soft plastic container hanging on a pole; by injection, which can be put directly into a specific area; and orally, in the form of pills. Oral chemotherapy is most popular with patients, since it is the easiest and most convenient way to administer the drug and the patient does not have to go to a doctor's office or hospital every time a dose is required.

But the other forms might be required for specific reasons. For instance, if the cancerous area is close enough to the body's surface the drugs can be injected directly into the site, or if getting the chemicals to go to work quickly is needed, the IV might be used since it puts the drugs directly into the bloodstream.

Hodgkin's patients frequently receive chemotherapy through an IV. The drugs are administered in several cycles. The ABVD drug combination, for instance, is given in four-week cycles. Two treatments, one every two weeks, makes up one cycle. The number of cycles will vary, but basically six cycles would consist of twelve ABVD treatments, each given two weeks apart. The patient goes to the hospital or clinic at the beginning of each cycle for treatments. Generally, chemotherapy is given over a period of one to three days, depending on the drugs the patient is receiving. Then, the patient is off of chemotherapy for a few weeks to allow the body to recover from the drugs' effects. Sometimes, the drugs are given in doctors' offices or clinics, but some chemotherapy drugs do require a hospital stay. The number of cycles of chemotherapy the patient has depends on several factors: which drugs the patient is receiving, the stage of Hodgkin's disease, test results, and how well the Hodgkin's is responding to treatment.

Chemotherapy attacks fast-growing cells. Unfortunately, chemotherapy cannot tell the difference between fast-growing cancer cells and other types of fast-growing cells, like hair, so these cells are damaged as well. This is what causes people's hair to fall out when they have this type of chemotherapy.

Sometimes patients have other side effects from chemotherapy as well, such as dry skin, sore mouth, nausea, loss of appetite, or diarrhea. Since some types of chemotherapy drugs affect both red and white blood cells, which help the body fight infection, the patient's immune system may be temporarily weakened and the patient might be more likely to catch colds and other communicable diseases. Sometimes patients are asked to avoid crowds like shopping malls or family gatherings during chemotherapy to lessen their chances of catching a cold or influenza. Also, patients may bruise more easily while they are receiving chemotherapy. Lowered blood cell count, which can cause anemia, and lack of sleep sometimes associated with chemotherapy can cause the patient to tire more easily. Another side effect of chemotherapy is a condition called neuropathy. With neuropathy, patients may experience tingling or numbness in hands and feet.

Writer Maureen McHugh described her experience with this condition during chemotherapy:

> Periodically I will experience something—I had a numbness and tingling in one hand and fingers after my first chemo, although it went away and never came back—and I will think, 'maybe I shouldn't do this chemo stuff.' And then it will occur to me that a little neuropathy beats the alternative.[6]

Chemotherapy may also affect the way some foods taste. While on chemotherapy, some people may stop eating certain favorite foods because of the way they taste. When chemotherapy is over, though, most people are able to enjoy the flavors of their favorite foods, just as they did prior to treatment.

Another important issue with chemotherapy patients is whether or not they may continue to take vitamin and mineral supplements while undergoing treatment. Many people take these substances to maintain and improve general health, however there are some vitamin and mineral supplements that may interfere with the effectiveness of chemotherapy. Patients need to discuss any vitamin or mineral supplements or any other substances they may be taking with their doctors. To make sure these supplements do not cause negative effects during chemotherapy, the medical team might ask the patient to refrain from taking them during the course of treatment.

Since the early days of nitrogen mustard, drugs used in chemotherapy have come a long way. Today, instead of a single drug, a group of drugs is usually administered to the patient

# Getting Healing from a Killer Chemical

Nitrogen mustard was once a weapon of chemical warfare and was stockpiled in many countries in the 1940s. Today, it is a potential agent of chemical terrorism. However, nitrogen mustard has another use, as well. It was the first drug used in chemotherapy to kill cancer in the 1940s.

Discovered by accident when victims of nitrogen mustard gas poisoning were autopsied, doctors noticed that the nitrogen mustard had an effect on the victims' lymphatic systems. Next, researchers tested it by creating lymphomas in mice, then treating the mice with nitrogen mustard. The tumor masses were reduced by the drug.

Although nitrogen mustard is not commonly used to treat cancer today, this deadly substance led the way in chemotherapy research.

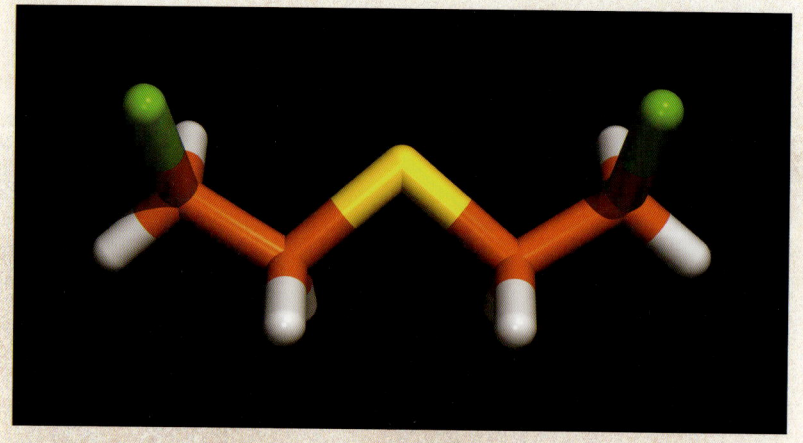

This computer graphic shows a molecule of mustard gas. This weapon of chemical warfare was the drug initially used in chemotherapy during the 1940s.

during chemotherapy. Each drug has different properties that when given together work as a powerful weapon against lymphoma. The names of the different drugs are frequently grouped together in an acronym, such as ABVD, for the drugs Adriamycin, Bleomycin, Vinblastine, and Dacarbazine, and VAMP, for Vinchristine, Adriamycin, Methotrexate, and Prednisone. The acronyms are much easier to say and to remember than the name of each drug in the group. The medical team carefully evaluates each patient to determine which grouping of drugs will work best for that individual.

## Radiation

Radiation therapy, also called X-ray therapy or radiotherapy, is the treatment of diseases such as cancer by exposure to powerful X-rays or other radioactive substances. It works by attacking the DNA of the cancer cells. The radiation breaks a strand of the DNA molecule, thereby preventing the cancer cells from growing or dividing. Unlike chemotherapy, which affects the entire body, radiation therapy affects only the tissues at which it is directed.

Radiation treatment began toward the end of the nineteenth century, when German physicist Wilhelm Roentgen discovered a type of energy he named the X-ray. While observing electron beams in his laboratory one day, he noticed that a fluorescent screen he had in the room glowed whenever he turned on the beam. Since the screen was surrounded by several layers of cardboard, Roentgen knew no outside light could reach it. He attempted to block the rays with his hand, and to his surprise he could see the silhouette of the bones of his hand on the screen. Roentgen discovered that X-rays are a form of radiation, which travels like light rays, but can travel through substances, like human flesh. The scientific community was quite excited by this discovery, because for the first time they could see inside the body. This would help in diagnosing medical conditions, such as types of cancer.

When it was first developed, though, radiation therapy was quite dangerous and often deadly, not only to the patients,

German physicist Wilhelm Roentgen discovered the type of energy known as X-rays. This energy also is used as radiation therapy to treat cancer such Hodgkin's disease.

# Treatments

but to the lab technicians as well. The scientists did not know that their repeated exposure to the X-rays as they used the devices on patients caused the technicians to develop radiation poisoning. In the earliest days of radiation therapy, scientists were not sure what was a safe amount of X-ray energy to use on patients. For instance, some patients suffered radiation burns to healthy tissue. For a time, it appeared that radiation therapy was more harmful than the cancer it was used to treat. Over time, though, technicians learned to protect themselves with lead-lined aprons and scientists were able to determine safe doses. Today, radiation therapy is a highly reliable form of treatment for Hodgkin's disease and many other forms of cancer.

Radiation therapy is sometimes used on its own and sometimes in conjunction with chemotherapy. The development of MRI and PET technology has made it possible to more effectively pinpoint tumors, which, in turn, has made radiation therapy more successful in treating many forms of cancer. In fact, radiation is very effective in treating certain types and stages of Hodgkin's disease. It is often given in early, localized stages of Hodgkin's lymphoma. In this type of treatment, high-energy X-rays are used to kill tiny cancer cells and shrink tumors.

The three main types of radiation therapy are external beam radiotherapy (EBRT), also called teletherapy, brachytherapy, or sealed source radiotherapy, and unsealed source radiotherapy. These names have to do with where the radiation's source is placed when it is used in treatment. External means the source of radiation is outside the body. Sealed and unsealed source radiotherapy, however, means the source is implanted into the body and the radiation is delivered internally. For treatments, brachytherapy sealed sources are usually implanted surgically while unsealed source radiation can be given by injection or the patient may swallow it.

Usually, Hodgkin's lymphoma is treated with external beam radiation therapy. This is a machine that beams radiation to the tumor from outside the body. Sometimes, though, bits of radioactive material, often called seeds, are put directly into tumors. The type of radiation a person will receive will be decided by a radiation oncologist, a specialist who works with radiation therapy. The oncologist will evaluate the patient's condition, the results of other tests, like scans and X-rays, and the patient's medical background to decide which type of treatment will be more effective.

Before radiation treatment begins, the oncologist will identify the parts of the body where the lymphoma are located. These areas are called treatment ports, or fields. If radiation is given to the neck, chest, or lymph nodes under the arms, this is called the mantle field. If radiation will be applied to the mantle field plus lymph nodes in the upper abdomen, the spleen, and the lymph nodes in the pelvis, this is called total nodal irradiation.

A patient receiving external beam radiation therapy at the Oscar Lambret Cancerology Center in Lille, France. This type of radiotherapy targets radiation to the tumor from outside the body and reduces the effects to the healthy tissue surrounding the tumor.

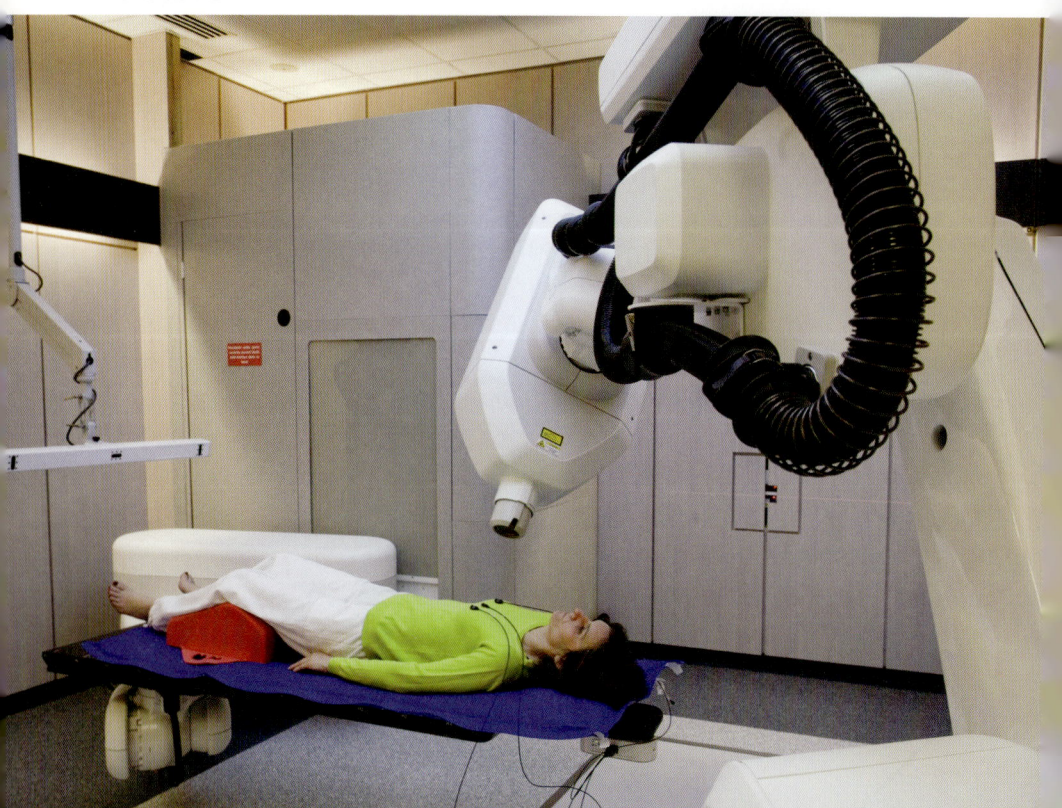

# Radioactive Seeds

Also called brachytherapy, radioactive seed implants are a relatively new method of delivering radiation to cancer cells. Rice-sized radioactive pellets, called seeds, are implanted into the lymphoma through hollow needles. Once implanted, the seeds usually are not removed. There is no danger with leaving in the seeds. They completely lose their radiation within one year.

Brachytherapy delivers a higher dose of radiation than external beam radiation, but delivers the dose to a smaller area, so it is more successful with smaller tumors. Although it has proven useful in the treatment of lymphoma, like other types of radiation treatment brachytherapy is not without side effects. Patients may experience loss of appetite and fatigue, but the symptoms should disappear within a couple of months.

The oncologist examines these areas in simulations. This may take an hour or two. At this time, the patient will be instructed to lie as still as possible on an X-ray table while the medical team pinpoints these areas in the body. Once they have the information, the oncologist can determine the appropriate amount of radiation to use. The oncologist wants to use the maximum dosage of radiation to kill the cancer cells without damaging surrounding tissue. Once the dosage is determined, the oncologist will divide it into smaller doses to be given over a period of several weeks. When the treatments begin, other parts of the body may be covered with special barriers to protect them from radiation. However, some healthy tissue might be affected due to small, involuntary body movement caused by normal body functions, such as breathing or filling of the bladder. Additionally, radiation beams may be directed into the tumor from several directions at the same time. The beams intersect at the tumor, which gives it a more directed dose of the radiation and spares surrounding healthy tissue.

As effective as radiation therapy is, though, it is not without possible short-term side effects. Sometimes the skin at the site may become pink and sore, like a sunburn, or the area may become swollen. The sunburn-like condition usually appears a few weeks into treatment. These skin reactions are usually more troublesome in areas where the skin naturally folds, like underneath the female breast and in the groin area. Although this condition may be uncomfortable, most patients recover quickly. If swelling is a problem, the medical team may give the patient steroids during the course of radiation in order to reduce the swelling.

Other side effects may be long-term and more serious, though. In later years, some patients may develop problems with their bone tissue, like osteoporosis. Others may have stomach problems. Additionally, in some instances, female patients who are treated between the ages of ten and sixteen might develop breast cancer when they become adults. Some types of radiation may cause infertility in both men and women. Finally, in a small minority of patients, other types of cancer may develop years after the radiation treatments. However, with all of the technologies and safeguards that have been developed in conjunction with modern radiation treatment, such problems are very rare.

## A Drug Alphabet

As patients and their families become involved in the treatment and recovery process, they encounter a whole new vocabulary, with names of drugs they will receive during their treatment spanning the alphabet. There are drugs for treatment, and drugs for relieving the side effects of the treatment drugs. Many such drugs have been developed over the years to treat Hodgkin's disease, as well as other forms of cancer.

As previously mentioned, due to the strength of these drugs and the way they react within the body, some cancer-treating drugs cause uncomfortable and unpleasant side effects including a drop in white or red blood cells, leading to a condition called anemia, skin irritation, hair loss, nausea, and possibly

# Treatments

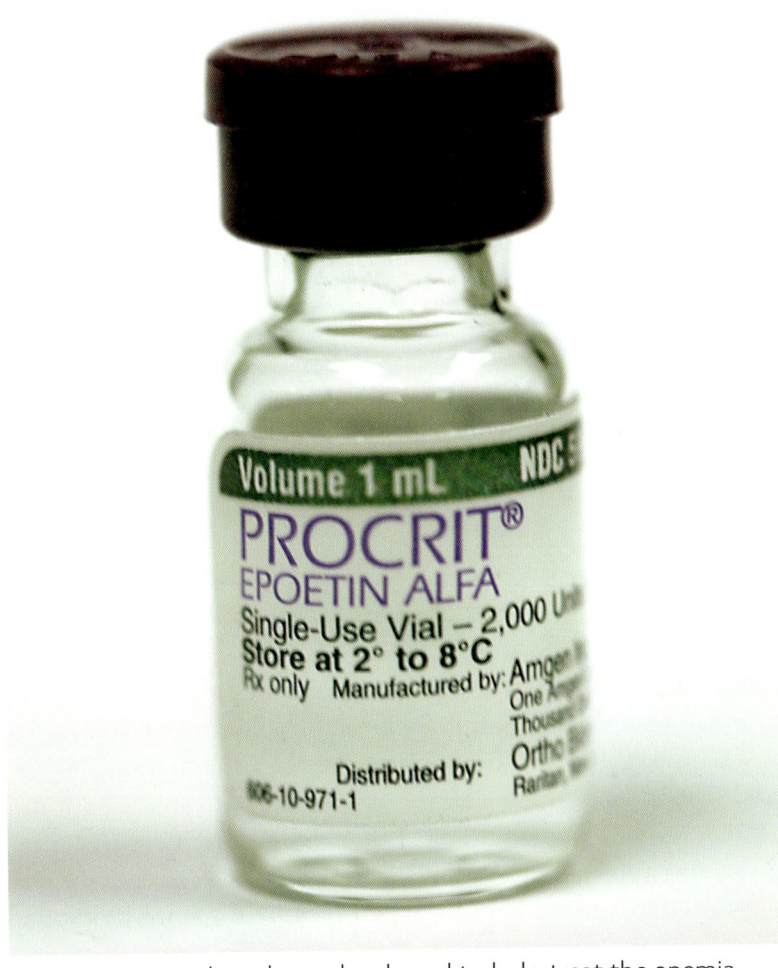

Drugs like Procrit have been developed to help treat the anemia experienced by Hodgkin's patients as a result of treatment with chemotherapy.

diarrhea and vomiting. A number of medications have been developed that can lessen or completely relieve these side effects. Zofran, also known as Kytril, helps relieve the nausea caused by chemotherapy. Procrit, or Epoetin, counteracts anemia by raising the red blood cell count. Another drug, Neupogen, raises the white blood cell count.

CHAPTER FOUR

# Alternative Therapies

Many doctors rely solely on chemotherapy, radiation, and other conventional forms of treatment for their Hodgkin's patients. However, some alternative therapies are also approved by the medical community. Some of these alternative therapies are used in conjunction with conventional treatment for the overall well-being of the patient. However, others of these so-called therapies are little more than what Americans of an earlier day would have called "snake oil." This means something that promises false hope and delivers nothing.

Patients who hear about some of these alternative therapies from friends or family members or read about them in the newspaper or over the Internet should be extremely cautious about pursuing them. If the patient is interested in trying one of these therapies, it should first be carefully discussed with the medical team in charge of the person's treatment. The patient may ask if the medical team recommends any types of alternative therapies or if there are any that they would advise against. Additionally, the patient would need to know if any alternative therapies are provided as a part of the medical team's practice, or if they would recommend an alternative therapy practitioner. Finally, the patient needs to know if any approved alternative therapies are covered by insurance.

It is important to fully discuss alternative therapies with the medical team because, while combining alternative therapies with conventional treatment can sometimes be helpful, there is also the danger that some of the substances used in the

# Alternative Therapies

# Ayurvedic Medicine

Ayurvedic comes from two words; Ayur, which means life, and veda, which means knowledge. Ayurvedic medicine is based on the traditional medicine of India. More than five thousand years old, Ayurvedic practices have been handed down by word of mouth. Most Ayurvedic treatments are herbal or dietary. Some people claim that Ayurvedic treatments are useful in preventing or curing cancer, however there are currently no clinical trails or other research recognized by the conventional medical community to support these claims. Because of this, physicians strongly recommend that Ayurveda should not be used in place of standard cancer therapies.

Although some people claim that using Ayurvedic spices, like the ones pictured here, are useful in preventing or curing cancer, physicians recommend that these spices should never be used in place of conventional treatments.

alternative therapy could have a negative effect on the drugs used in conventional treatment. Additionally, anyone who abruptly ceases conventional treatment in favor of alternative therapy places his or her health at grave risk.

In addition to discussing alternative therapies with the medical team, the patient should make every effort to be self-informed. The Internet provides some valuable resources about potentially dangerous or ineffective alternative therapies. One of these sources is Dr. Stephen Barrett's *QwackWatch*. This site includes a section about alternative cancer treatments.

## What are CAM Therapies?

CAM, also called integrated medicine, stands for complementary and alternative medicine. Complementary therapies are used in conjunction with, and in support of, conventional medicine whereas alternative treatments usually means instead of conventional medicine. In the case of Hodgkin's disease and

At once thought to be harmful to cancer patients, it is now believed that massages can help to ease stress and physical pain if the massage therapist has had special training in how to work with people with cancer.

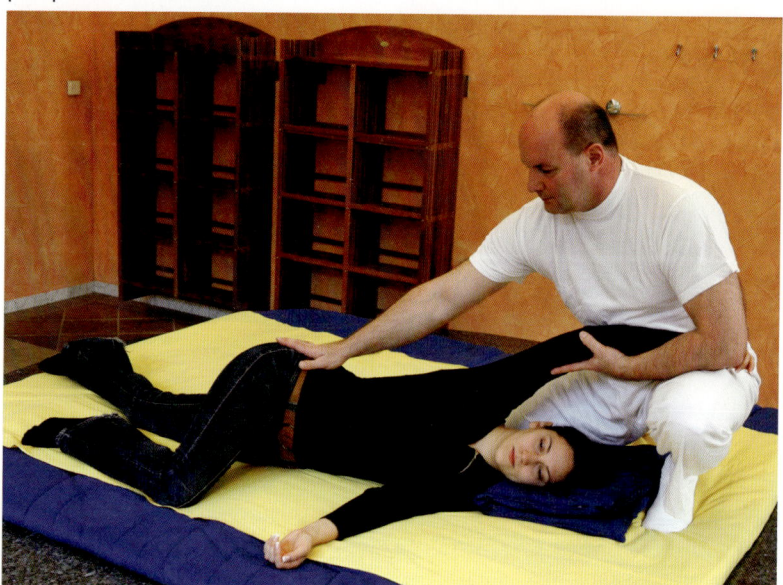

## Alternative Therapies

other forms of cancer, patients are often advised to rely more on conventional medicine and possibly consider using complementary therapies in support of their conventional treatments, if they are first approved by the medical team. Some of these complementary therapies have been studied and thoroughly evaluated and some have not. These therapies are intended to help manage symptoms, reduce side effects, and encourage a sense of control over one's health. CAM therapies include therapeutic massage, acupuncture, aroma therapy, and art and music therapy. The purpose of CAM therapies is to address not only the patient's body, but the mind and spirit as well, and to encourage the patient to be a partner in his or her treatment process.

For many years, the medical community warned against using massage in conjunction with cancer treatment. There was some thought that since Hodgkin's occurs in the lymphatic system and massage therapy increases the flow of blood and lymphatic fluids, then massage might spread cancer throughout the patient's body. However, there has been no medical evidence to prove this claim. Now, however, massage therapists can receive special training to work with cancer patients. Therapists are taught to place patients in positions that do not put pressure on surgical wounds and to avoid areas of the body near wounds, areas tender from radiation treatment, or known locations of lymphoma. Massage therapy eases stress and physical pain, two issues that can slow a cancer patient's recovery.

In addition to relieving pain and stress, some of these therapies appear to be effective in relieving chemotherapy symptoms, such as fatigue, nausea, and vomiting. However, there is presently no scientific evidence that CAM therapies slow the progression of Hodgkin's disease or any other type of cancer. Therefore, it is important to understand that CAM therapies are not cures. They should be used in conjunction with conventional treatment, not in place of it.

Some people say aromatherapy improves their moods and relieves stress. Aromatherapy is the use of essential oils, liquid plant material, and other substances to improve physical and mental well-being. Although this therapy did not become widely recognized in the United States until recent years, it was first developed in France in the 1920s. A French chemist, Rene Maurice Gattefosse, burned his arm in a laboratory accident. Supposedly, the only cool substance nearby Gattefosse could find to ease the burning was a vat of lavender oil. The chemist dipped his arm in the vat, and noticed almost immediate relief from the pain. According to the story, his arm healed quickly with less scarring than is usually experienced in such accidents.

For cancer patients, though, the oils are not used as an ointment or salve for physical injury, but rather for psychological benefits. According to some people, certain scents have helpful properties. For instance, basil is said to help relieve depression, the scent of lavender calms and relaxes, and lemon oil is a stress-reliever. As with any other type of alternative therapy, though, aroma therapy should be thoroughly discussed with the patient's medical team before pursuing it.

Of the CAM therapies discussed here, the only one that is actually physically invasive is acupuncture. Acupuncture is an ancient Chinese medical technique that involves inserting and manipulating fine needles at certain points in the body. Some patients report that acupuncture relieves the nausea caused by chemotherapy. This medical technique has been investigated by the American Medical Association (AMA), as well as other medical groups. It is generally agreed that although it does not cure cancer, acupuncture is a safe therapy, provided it is administered by a qualified practitioner.

Organizations such as the Leukemia and Lymphoma Society can provide helpful information about these treatments. Furthermore, in 1998 the National Institute of Health (NIH) founded the National Center for Complementary and Alternative Medicine (NCCAM) to investigate how CAM therapies work and to evaluate their effectiveness with Hodgkin's disease and other medical and psychological conditions. In this way, CAM therapies are subjected to the same strict scientific

# Alternative Therapies

investigation processes that are used to evaluate conventional cancer treatments. At this time, clinical trials are being conducted to try to determine if some of these therapies do actually improve the effects of conventional treatment, boost the immune system, and reduce the risk of developing cancer or the possibility that the cancer might return.

## Nutrition

Nutritional therapy does not cure cancer, but good nutrition is a vitally important part of a patient's overall treatment program. No one can deny that a healthy diet is important for everyone, sick or well. When a person is undergoing treatments such as chemotherapy or radiation, however, such issues as nausea, the effect these treatments have on the sense of taste, and even the smells of foods can seriously diminish the appetite. Other side effects that might affect the patient's appetite include sore or dry mouth, dental or gum problems, and not being able to digest milk products. Despite these drawbacks, though, patients need to maintain healthy eating habits

Experts agree that it is important for Hodgkin's patients to maintain a healthy and well-balanced diet before, during, and after treatment if they want to maintain their strength and overcome their illness.

before, during, and after treatments if they are to maintain their strength and overall well-being.

On the other hand, some people experience few if any of these side effects, but for those who do, there are medications available to help control the side effects so the person can maintain a healthy diet and lifestyle. The most important thing to keep in mind, though, is that even if a person is experiencing side effects that interfere with eating and other activities, the side effects go away when the treatment ends and the patient is able to return to a normal diet and enjoy favorite foods.

To help with any dietary issues, the medical team may have a nutritionist work with the patient. As with any other treatments, patients should keep a written record of foods normally eaten and any changes in tastes or appetite they experience so that all issues can be discussed with the dietitian during appointments. Each patient's needs are examined separately, but a dietitian will frequently recommend a diet high in fruits and vegetables and whole grain breads and cereals. Fats, sugar, alcohol, salt, and high fiber foods, which might irritate the stomach, should be kept to a minimum. Also, to maintain weight, the dietitian may recommend high calorie, high protein foods, sauces, gravies, cream, cheese, butter, and cooked eggs.

Although most patients work with their dietitians and stick with this more mainstream diet, some people follow a macrobiotic diet. As with any type of alternative therapy, if a patient is interested in trying a macrobiotic diet, this should be discussed with the medical team first. A macrobiotic diet is one that centers on grains and vegetables, but also includes beans, fish, fruits, fowl, seeds, and nuts. Most of these foods, including the fruits, are cooked.

According to the macrobiotic belief, foods range across a spectrum with animal meats at one end, root vegetables, whole grains and cereals in the middle, and fruits, refined sugars, and alcohol at the opposite end. People who practice this form of nutrition believe that eating too many foods from one end of the spectrum causes cravings for foods at the other end, and this leaves the body out of balance and vulnerable to stress and disease. They believe that focusing on foods in the middle of the spectrum helps maintain strength and energy.

Macrobiotic counselors recommend basing the diet on 50 to 60 percent whole grains and cereals, 25 to 30 percent on green vegetables, and the remainder from beans, tea, soups, and sea vegetables, like edible seaweeds. Fish and fruit should be eaten in small amounts and nuts and seeds limited to snacks. Dairy products, like cheese and milk, and eggs are strongly discouraged. The foods eaten should be fresh, not heavily processed, and cooked over gas or wood fires, not microwave or electricity.

Macrobiotic followers also believe that food should be prepared and eaten in a calm, peaceful setting and chewed until liquid before swallowing. This part of the macrobiotic belief, at least, is in total agreement with what people have heard their own mothers say at dinner tables for generations, "No arguments at mealtime and chew your food before you swallow it!"[7]

Despite the fact that the macrobiotic diet appears to be a healthy and sensible approach to nutrition, people, especially cancer patients, must be aware of the limitations of this diet. The macrobiotic diet can be deficient in nutrients that are especially important for cancer patients to maintain optimal health, such as protein, vitamins D and B12, and calcium and iron. The diet is also not recommended for patients who have experienced extreme weight loss. In fact, the American Cancer Society has remarked that a strict macrobiotic diet does not provide adequate nutrition for cancer patients, and there is a lack of clinical trial information about the usefulness of the macrobiotic diet for people undergoing cancer treatment.

## Yoga and Other Forms of Exercise

In addition to diet, exercise is an important factor in the Hodgkin's patient's overall well-being. Clinical studies performed over the past twelve to fifteen years have determined that moderate exercise is beneficial in the healing process for patients with Hodgkin's disease as well as other serious medical conditions. Exercise helps cancer patients in a variety of ways.

Walking is one of the best exercises for Hodgkin's patients to maintain their strength during treatment.

## Alternative Therapies

It relieves stress and lifts the patient's mood. It makes the person feel more in control when health issues are out of control. Exercise also builds strength and relieves fatigue.

If a person is normally athletic, these activities may be continued during treatment, but on a reduced or modified scale, because chemotherapy and radiation do weaken the body. However, people involved in extreme sports, such as mountain climbing, may have to substitute strength and agility-building exercises during treatment and take their time and work back up to these activities safely following treatment. In fact, it is important to maintain an exercise regimen both during and following treatments. For instance, if a person is normally involved in a weight training program, it may be necessary to use lesser weights and do fewer repetitions until the body recovers from the treatment process.

Dr. Anna Schwartz discussed issues such as weight, repetitions, and form in her book, *Cancer Fitness*, ". . . I have emphasized the importance of doing the exercises correctly and focusing on the quality, not the quantity, of your exercise. More is not better: proper form is what's important."[8]

Moderate exercise can help reduce nausea and neuropathy, a numbness or tingling in feet and hands some patients experience during chemotherapy and radiation treatments. People undergoing treatment need to understand that the goals of exercise during treatment are different than those of other times. Rather than body building or training for marathons, Hodgkin's patients are working to maintain strength, agility, and well-being for normal everyday activities, like going to work, grocery shopping, or taking a walk in the park. In fact, walking and riding a bicycle are good exercises for maintaining strength in the large muscle groups as well as aerobic fitness. Swimming is another excellent aerobic activity. Swimming is good for the heart and promotes overall muscle tone and fitness. If a person has had surgery, though, the incision needs time to heal properly before swimming is added to the exercise program. In fact, many experts recommend thirty minutes or more of moderate aerobic exercise daily for patients undergoing treatment, and the exercise can even be broken down into two or three short periods. However, a person should not be discouraged if there are days when exercise is just too uncomfortable. After all, there is always tomorrow.

Yoga is an ancient form of exercise that may be helpful to Hodgkin's patients. Many people discover the benefits of yoga during their cancer treatments. Yoga originated in India thousands of years ago. Although in its strictest sense yoga is a way of life, a highly disciplined combination of meditation and complicated movements and postures, for average people today yoga is the practice of asanas, or postures, which help improve mobility, flexibility, and overall strength. Another thing some people like about yoga is that it does not require expensive equipment, just a thick rug or a mat for the floor and comfortable clothing for moving through the postures. Although people can get an idea about what these postures look like from the Internet or a book, as with any other form of exercise, to avoid injury, these yoga postures must be practiced correctly. Anyone interested in pursuing yoga should check

## Quackery vs. Cure

People with Hodgkin's disease and their families are sometimes in a highly vulnerable state. They may feel that treatment is going too slowly or they may not be getting the results they want. Under some circumstances, people feel desperate enough to try anything that promises a cure, whether that promise can be backed up, or not.

In 2004, the Memorial Sloan-Kettering Cancer Center in New York reviewed the claims of a number of so-called cancer cures ranging from coffee enemas to extracts made from apricot pits and found them to be useless. To date, conventional treatments offer Hodgkin's patients the most hope because they have been thoroughly tested and found to have the highest success rates.

# Alternative Therapies

on classes at local health centers or colleges and learn from a qualified instructor.

All of these exercises are for people who are able to be out of bed. However, there are also some exercises Hodgkin's patients can do even if they are still recovering from surgery and are restricted to bed rest. These include breathing exercises, modified leg and knee lifts, ankle circles, and arm presses. As passive as they seem, though, these are exercises. To lessen the risk of injury, it is best if the patient and the caregiver are instructed in these exercises by a qualified physical therapist.

From bed exercises, the patient will progress to chair exercises. These movements include leg lifts, resistance exercises with a partner, and biceps curls performed with light weights. Finally, the patient will be ready for strength and balance exercises, like wall push-ups, partner pull-ups, and knee and leg exercises while holding a chair.

Patients who have undergone surgery or are on chemotherapy need to remember that recovery is a gradual process and should not be rushed. It will take time to return to the type of exercise and physical activities they pursue, but in the end, care and patience will be worth the effort.

## Visualization and Meditation

Not all recovery efforts are physical, however. Visualization therapy is a form of self-hypnosis or meditation that people can use to improve their physical and emotional well-being. It is like a mental spring cleaning, only instead of cleaning trash, dirt, dust, and unwanted items out of the house, patients clear unwanted depressing, stressful, or angry thoughts from their minds and replace them with positive thoughts. In visualization therapy, the patient imagines positive outcomes to situations or events, such as successful surgery or chemotherapy.

In an article titled "Visualisation Therapy," psychologist Emile Coue described the mental battle of positive over negative thoughts, "In a battle between willpower and imagination, imagination will always win."[9]

People who practice visualization therapy techniques believe that everyone can imagine their way to improved physical and mental health. Active imagery is just as the name implies; active mental images. For instance, a person may imagine an army platoon in his body, attacking lymphoma and destroying it. Some studies indicate that this type of mental activity actually increases the production of immune cells that attack cancer. Additionally, it is said to relieve stress and depression, help control pain, and overall improve quality of life.

As with other complementary therapies, mental exercise, whether it is called meditation, self-hypnosis, or active imagery, gives patients a sense of being in charge of their own lives, even when some parts of their lives, like their health, seem out of control.

Finally, many cancer patients who follow religious teachings find peace, well-being, and comfort in their faith and prayer. Prayer can be a spiritual support system, with many different groups conducting prayer services, sometimes called healing services, based on the requests of members for themselves, their family members, or their friends. Prayer does not have to be a group activity, though. Anyone of any faith can find comfort through private prayer.

## CHAPTER FIVE

# Living and Coping

Getting through the treatment and recovery process may require rethinking and readjusting a person's concept of a normal life, at least temporarily. For most people, normal is getting up every morning and going to school or work. Afterwards, some people participate in after school or after work activities, come home and have dinner, do homework, perhaps relax for a while by listening to music or watching a television program, and then going to bed to repeat the routine the next day. However, normal life for people undergoing treatment for Hodgkin's disease requires a number of modifications. These include arranging time for medical and treatment appointments, learning about drugs that must be taken during treatment, finding a quiet place for rest when feeling ill, and dealing with the emotional issues that go along with a serious illness. One issue that affects many people is the temporary changes in their physical appearance caused by surgery, radiation, or chemotherapy.

## Coping with Changes in Physical Appearance

People facing chemotherapy are concerned not only about feeling ill, but also about changes in the way they look. In her book *Beauty Therapy*, makeup artist Ramy Gafni described these feelings from personal experience:

> When people are being treated for cancer, their self-image is often shattered. Cancer treatments are both a blessing

and a curse. The very treatment that can save your life can also change your physical appearance, sometimes in traumatic ways. Suddenly, not only are you fighting for your life, but you are doing it while a stranger is staring back at you from the mirror . . .[10]

For instance, chemotherapy attacks fast-growing cancer cells and kills them. This is exactly what it is supposed to do. However, chemotherapy does not know the difference between fast-growing cancer cells and fast-growing hair cells, so many people lose their hair during chemotherapy. While it is disturbing for men to lose their hair, it can be especially disturbing to women, teens, and children. Some cancer patients feel as though they are marked, or singled out, by their change in appearance, as though they are carrying a sign that says, "Stare at me. Treat me differently. I have cancer." Physical appearance is another area where a person's idea about what is normal may need to change, at least during the treatment period.

A worker at a hospital in Garden City, Kansas, demonstrates to a cancer patient how to draw on eyebrows lost during chemotherapy. Programs like this are important in helping cancer patients improve their self-image and self-esteem during treatment.

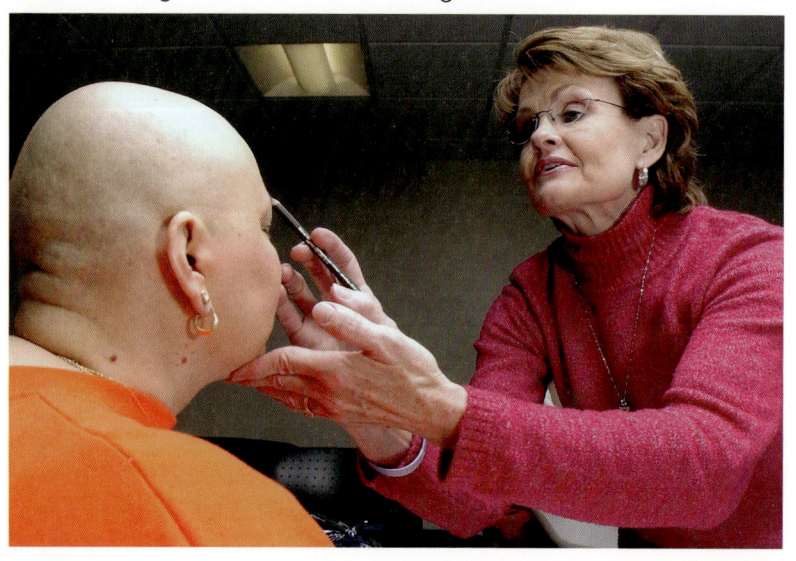

## Living and Coping

For many women, the rituals of applying makeup or indulging in a facial are normal, routine activities. These activities are especially important while undergoing treatment, when the skin can be dry, look pasty, and eyes may be ringed with dark circles. Continuing beauty habits during chemotherapy can help improve self-image and self-esteem and can make a person feel more positive and in control. The goal of a beauty regimen during cancer treatment is not to look like a super model, but rather to look as healthy as possible. Women undergoing treatment for any kind of cancer have unique needs. Some skin care experts recommend skin exfoliating products containing fruity acids to gently remove the outer layer of dead, dry, flaky skin cells, revealing the healthy skin underneath. These products diminish fine lines and leave the skin with a rosy glow. For especially sensitive skin, a product with 2 percent or less alpha-hydroxy, used every other day, is the safest choice.

Both men and women could benefit from facial scrubs while they are undergoing treatment. Facial scrubs remove dead skin and improve blood circulation in the face. A scrub is also good for the scalp, if the patient has lost hair. Like exfoliants, many of these scrubs contain fruit acids. Some also contain vitamins A and C. Other facial scrubs contain soothing ingredients, like chamomile or cucumber. If a person has extra sensitive skin and the tiny scrubbing beads are irritating, another option is an exfoliating mask, a cream that removes the dead skin cells by sticking to them as the cream dries on the skin. When the cream is completely dry, it is easily rinsed off, removing both the products and the dead skin cells.

Since dry skin is a side effect of chemotherapy, moisturizers are important for men, women, children, and teens. Moisturizers are applied to the face and the body right after baths and showers first thing in the morning to seal moisture into the skin. Sometimes, bathing is an issue of its own. If a person is undergoing radiation therapy, there may be some areas of red, sensitive skin. A mild soap and a soft sponge will help prevent further skin irritation.

In addition to using moisturizers after baths, these products can also be applied at night, so they can be working as the person sleeps. Men and boys will be relieved to discover that many good moisturizers come unscented or scented like aftershave products, so they will not have to go through the day trailing a flowery or fruity scent.

One product that has been developed fairly recently is the tinted moisturizer. Tinted moisturizers have a two-fold purpose. They moisturize the skin and add a hint of healthy color. Some women now use tinted moisturizers instead of applying both moisturizers and foundations. Many men use this product, as well. They appreciate the healthy skin tone tinted moisturizers help create.

Skin care should be practiced on a daily basis. A person should begin with a good facial cleanser, used according to directions, then apply the correct moisturizing product for the individual's skin type. Then, if dark circles are a problem, an under-eye moisturizing concealer, about a shade lighter than normal skin tone, can be applied all around the eyes, carefully smoothing it into the skin, to avoid a reverse raccoon look. These first steps are as important for men as they are for women.

Once basic skin care has been attended to for the day, some women may opt to apply makeup. Women with facial blemishes, discoloration, or uneven skin tone, whether their skin is normally that way or the result of chemotherapy, may begin with a foundation. Makeup foundations come in creams, powders, liquids, or sticks. To choose a good foundation, apply a sample to the jaw line and blend it in. When dried, foundation should virtually disappear. Next, some women apply bronzers. Bronzers should be applied to any part of the face the sun would normally color. Like foundation, it is a good idea to remember that a little bronzer goes a long way. Finally, blushers may be lightly applied to the apple of the cheeks, the area that would be naturally colored by the sun.

Eye makeup may become especially important to women who have lost their hair. Eyeliner should be applied close to

# Self-Image

Cancer treatment can affect a person's self-image. This is because the person is undergoing both physical and emotional changes. Chemotherapy can leave a person feeling fuzzy-headed and too tired to deal with such things as grocery shopping and cooking, and facing an unknown future can be frightening and depressing. It can also be depressing to look in a mirror and see a stranger with dry, blotchy skin and thinning hair looking back.

Patients can plan in advance to deal with some of these issues. For instance, if the person is facing a type of chemotherapy that causes hair loss, that person may want to get a short haircut or even shave the head entirely, so hair will not be falling on clothing and furniture. If the person is uncomfortable with a bald head, hats, scarves, and wigs are available.

Families and friends can organize support systems for dealing with shopping, cooking, and other chores while the patient is feeling weak from treatments. Also, it is important to stay as active as possible, getting out of bed and dressing for the day, shaving, or putting on makeup. A good self-image is empowering.

Head scarves and wigs are good ways to deal with the hair loss patients experience as a result of the chemotherapy used to treat cancer.

the root line of the upper lashes. This gives the appearance of eyelashes. Blending a shadow one shade lighter than the eyeliner will add additional definition to the eyes. Eyebrows should be lightly penciled in with a feathering technique, to mimic the individual hairs in the eyebrows. If eyebrows are heavily drawn on, they can make the face look artificial and cartoon-like. There are a number of eye makeup products specifically for women who have lost their hair to chemotherapy or illness. Some makeup artists recommend a product called Miracle Brow.

When it comes to lipsticks, women should stick to whatever colors and products they usually use. Some women prefer cream formulas while others prefer sheer lipsticks, glosses, or lip balms. Any lipstick or balm that adds moisture is a good choice.

One thing men and women who lose hair from chemotherapy have to decide is whether to wear wigs or go natural. Many

Hospital staff helping a cancer patient choose a wig. There are several organizations around the United States that provide cancer patients with wigs in order to improve self-confidence during treatment.

modern wigs, hair pieces, and toupees look completely natural and no one will know if the person wearing the wig is sporting his or her own hair, or not. Counselors at the treatment centers can suggest specific products, but there is an organization that specializes in providing hair for underprivileged children and teens. Locks of Love is a nonprofit organization that provides natural or synthetic hairpieces for financially disadvantaged young people under the age of eighteen. The hairpieces are either provided free or on a sliding scale, based on financial need. Locks of Love receives donations of real hair from volunteers. From this natural hair, they create high quality hair prosthetics. The goal of Locks of Love is to help young people regain their self-confidence.

Some patients choose to forgo wigs in favor of colorful, stylish scarves, hats, and head wraps. Many large cancer treatment centers have head covering boutiques on site where patients can try on these products, just like trying on a dress at a department store. Sales associates are on hand to teach customers how to wrap and secure the head coverings in a variety of ways.

However, the most important factor in physical appearance has nothing to do with skin products, makeup, or wigs. A positive attitude enhances a person's appearance from the inside out. Part of a positive attitude is people's ability to accept themselves as they are at that particular time and to make the best of the situation.

## Coping as a Family

The family can be a big help in supporting the patient's attitude and self-acceptance. Many changes occur in the family's routine when a family member is diagnosed with Hodgkin's disease. Visits to hospitals and doctors' offices, treatment procedures, medications, and rest and recovery periods must be incorporated into the daily routine. Occasionally, an adult family member will take some vacation time or a leave of absence from work in order to be available to take the family member with Hodgkin's to these appointments and to help with side effects of treatments. Brothers and sisters may have to temporarily give up some after school activities because of these appointments or may need to pitch in and help around the house more than they normally do. Sometimes, working cooperatively for the welfare of a family member brings the rest of the family closer together.

To help with their loved one's recovery, family members may have to sacrifice more than their time. For instance, if the patient has an upstairs bedroom and a brother or sister has a downstairs bedroom, that person may have to change bedrooms because the patient may experience physical weakness during chemotherapy or radiation and might not feel strong enough to walk up and down the stairs to his or her bedroom for a while. Sometimes, if there is not a downstairs bedroom, the living room or den may become the patient's bedroom until he or she is through with treatment.

Mealtimes may change, as well. While undergoing treatment, the patient's appetite is often affected. Also, the person might be placed on a special diet or may not be able to tolerate

It is important that Hodgkin's patients have a support group of family and friends to help them cope with the disease.

## Living and Coping

the smell of foods the family usually enjoys. Some foods may have to be set aside during the patient's treatment. Parents may have less time to cook, so older children may take on some of the kitchen duties. Otherwise, the family may see a steady diet of take-out foods while the person is undergoing treatment.

Other issues may make brothers and sisters feel resentful. They may not be able to have friends over to visit, because the patient needs to rest and cannot have a lot of noise in the house. There is also the problem of infection. The more people who come around the house, the more likely the patient, in this weakened state, can catch a variety of communicable diseases. The family member needs peace and quiet and a healthy environment in order to get well.

One parent named Ellen praised her other children's willingness to cooperate while their brother was undergoing treatment.

> The boys understood and accepted this well. They knew how delicate Alex's immune system was after seeing him suffer through so many infections. Not only did they comply with the restrictions to visits from their friends at home, they didn't push for visiting Alex whenever he was hospitalized for infections.[11]

Additionally, treatment can be very costly, especially if the family has little or no health insurance. Limited finances might mean less money for new clothes, birthday and holiday gifts, family vacations, and fees for sports organizations. It is important to remember at this time that the family member did not deliberately get sick, and has no control over the changes in family routine and finances.

Another hardship some families face when a family member needs treatment is separation. If this is the case, the family member may have to stay in another city for a while. If the family member needing treatment is one of the children, a parent will have to go along to stay with the child until the treatment is completed. Sometimes, the other parent is able to cope with the

# Importance of Support Groups

Support groups do not work for everyone, but they do offer many cancer patients and their families resources to get them through the difficulties associated with cancer treatment. A support group is a place a person can go for emotional support and as a source of useful information. It is a place to share experiences with others who are involved in similar conditions. Although each individual's experience is unique, support groups do address many of the issues cancer patients and their families confront during their period of treatment and recovery.

Members of cancer support groups tend to live longer and have a higher quality of life, because these groups help patients and their families deal with stress and other emotional issues. Stress can affect the immune system and inhibit the recovery process.

family situation at home. Sometimes, though, the children might have to go stay with a relative or family friend until treatment is finished and the family can be back together again. It may even be necessary to transfer to another school for a few months. This can be frightening and unsettling, especially for younger children who may fear their parents and siblings are never coming back. It is important to frequently reassure the younger children that the rest of the family will be coming home and they will be together again. This responsibility can be taken on by an older brother or sister. It will also help if parents stay in frequent contact by phone and email. Additionally, school counselors should be notified when family changes like these take place so the school can be part of the child's support system.

# Living and Coping

## Support Organizations

In addition to help from family, friends, and school, people with Hodgkin's and their families need other types of support. The Lymphoma Support Foundation (LSF) is an organization devoted to assisting patients and their families in a variety of ways. For people who do not have a support chapter in their area, LSF sponsors on-line education programs, webcasts, teleconferences, radio programs, and even iPod presentations. To raise money for research, LSF sponsors golf tournaments, bike rides, and walks called Lymphomathons. Additionally, a Broadway gala was held in the fall of 2007 to raise money for lymphoma research. For competitive athletes, a marathon for lymphoma research and education was held in Sedona, Arizona, in 2008.

As important as programs are for Hodgkin's patients and research, family members need help as well. One organization that addresses the needs of brothers and sisters of disabled people and people with special health needs is called the Sibling Support Project. This group promotes the awareness of and provides support groups, educational materials, Web sites, and newsletters for siblings of people with special needs. Workshops, called Sibshops, are held in all fifty states to address the issues of living and interacting with a disabled sibling or a sibling with serious health issues.

One of the most comprehensive support organizations for patients with all types of cancer, though, is the American Cancer Society. Among other efforts, the American Cancer Society sponsors a Web site that includes a wide variety of information for patients and their families involved with all types of cancer. The site supplies information on patient education, the latest treatment techniques, and the importance of early detection screening. The site also supplies information about maintaining a healthy lifestyle before, during, and after treatment, including exercise and nutrition information. Additionally, patients and their families can go to this site to obtain information about lodging and transportation if they are preparing to have treatment in other cities.

Some treatment centers even have residential facilities for patients' families either at the center or near it. One of the best-known is the Ronald McDonald House Charities. This organization builds rest areas in hospitals, called Ronald McDonald Family Rooms, where families can briefly escape the stresses of the hospital setting. One hundred of these family rooms have been installed in hospitals in eleven countries. The organization also supports Ronald McDonald House, a home-away-from-home setting for families of children from infants to age twenty-one. Families can stay in these homes as long as they need, whether they need a place to stay overnight or for a year or more. If they can afford it, families are asked to donate $5 to $20 per day for their stay. However, if they cannot afford it, they may stay at no cost.

Emotional and financial support are important considerations and the lack of such support systems can be real stumbling blocks during the patient's treatment and recovery program. Although patients and their families can research information about support groups on the Internet, most medical teams can supply patients and their families with a list of local support groups and information to help them with such issues as counseling, lodging and transportation, and financial assistance.

CHAPTER SIX

# Today's Cutting Edge and Looking Ahead

When it comes to medicine and science, yesterday's science fiction is today's fact and something that exists only in theory today could be tomorrow's reality. Thanks to the ongoing research of scientists and physicians, knowledge about how Hodgkin's and other cancers behave in the body is growing rapidly. This includes the makeup of individual cancer cells and how these cells respond to different substances. Because of research developments, medical treatments that seem radical today may be commonplace in a few years' time.

For instance, many people have seen the old science fiction film *Fantastic Voyage*, about a medical team that boards a small submarine, which is shrunk down to a tiny speck. The microscopic submarine is then injected into the neck of a man who has a blood clot in his brain. Although surgeons are not being shrunk and injected into arteries to perform surgery inside of patients today, many patients are treated for cancer and a variety of diseases through microsurgery.

In a fictional story written in the late 1990s, an American surgeon performed operations on three different continents in the same day using a technique called remote site surgery. One of these surgeries was a lymph node transplant, performed on a Hodgkin's patient. Just a dozen or so years later, however, the idea of remote site surgery does not seem quite

Although surgeons are not yet being shrunk and injected into people, like in the film *Fantastic Voyage*, physicians are using microsurgery to treat cancer, like Hodgkin's disease.

so unbelievable. In fact, the science of telerobitics is getting a great deal of attention, and has already been used in some procedures, with robots performing according to the directions of surgeons hundreds of miles away.

## Boosting the Immune System

At one time, the idea of drugs helping the body's immune system repel or destroy different types of cancer was something seen only in futuristic movies. Such an idea was pure science fiction. However, scientists have taken this idea and put it to work. They are proving that the body can be helped to reject Hodgkin's disease and other types of cancer. In addition to cures from outside the body, cells within the body may prove useful in curing cancer. The immune system is made up of special protective cells called leukocytes. These cells protect the body from all kinds of foreign matter, or antigens. Foreign matter includes bacteria, parasites, and viruses. Proteins, called antibodies, are produced by the immune system. These

## Today's Cutting Edge and Looking Ahead

antibodies attach to the antigens and, with the help of other cells in the immune system, work together to destroy the antigens. These antibodies are being carefully studied for use in cancer treatment.

Additionally, research is underway today to develop drugs, tailor made for individual patients, by using information from the DNA of individual patients. In fact, drugs are already being developed today using DNA information. These drugs act like security systems, quickly identifying bits of DNA found in bacteria, viruses, and tumors. The drugs are called CG DNA, and can actually activate and boost the body's immune response system, attacking tumors.

While these drugs are still largely in experimental use, some anticancer vaccines are much farther along in development. There are two categories of anticancer vaccines, therapeutic and prophylactic. Therapeutic vaccines treat Hodgkin's disease and other types of cancer that already exist in the body. Prophylactic vaccines are vaccines designed to prevent different types of cancer from developing.

Immunotherapy, or biological therapy, uses the body's own immune system to fight cancer. These drugs work with the immune system to protect the body from foreign invaders. Immunotherapy strengthens the immune system and makes it function more effectively in several ways. It makes cancer cells more recognizable so the immune system can destroy them. Immunotherapy boosts the killing power of the body's natural cancer-fighting cells, such as B-cells, which, when they come into contact with abnormal cells, such as cancer cells, produce antibodies that attack the cells, and T-cells, which directly attack cancer cells, punching holes in them. It also keeps normal cells from mutating into cancer cells, changes the way existing cancer cells grow, so they behave more like healthy cells, and prevents cancer from spreading.

There are several types of immunotherapy. Among them are nonspecific immunomodulating agents and biological response modifiers, or BRMs. Immunomodulating agents stimulate the immune system to fight cancer and infection. BRMs strengthen the immune system, enhance the body's ability to fight disease, and direct the immune system to diseased cells, like cancer cells.

Among BRMs are monoclonal antibodies, which are laboratory-produced substances that bind with cancer cells and attract cancer-destroying cells. By attracting the cancer-destroying cells directly to the cancer, nearby healthy cells are not destroyed. Cytokine therapy is another form of BRM. In cytokine therapy, proteins called cytokines are used to help the immune system recognize and destroy cancerous cells. The body's immune system produces cytokines, but they can also be created in the laboratory. In cytokine therapy, all parts of the body are reached by these special proteins, which kill cancerous cells and prevent growth of tumors.

Vaccine therapy is still largely an experimental therapy. Although the benefits of vaccine therapy have not been thoroughly examined, this therapy carries high hopes among the medical community. Cancer vaccines are given after the condition develops, but while the involved area is still small. Vaccine may be combined with other types of cancer therapy to improve the quality of treatment and increase the chances that the cancer will be completely destroyed throughout the body.

T-cell immunotherapy, however, is a new type of immunotherapy that is just going into clinical trials, which will require several years. This is not the beginning of the work of developing this new treatment, however. Scientists have already been studying and researching T-cells as a type of treatment for about ten years. In theory, T-cell immunotherapy consists of removing the body's T-lymphocytes, taking them to the laboratory to be multiplied and modified, and then placed back into the patient's body where these modified and improved cells will attack lymphoma and other types of cancer.

As with other forms of treatment, some people experience many side effects from these vaccines, some have few, and some have no side effects at all. These side effects are essentially the same as those of chemotherapy, such as fever, nausea, vomiting, loss of appetite, fatigue, and chills.

## Stem Cell and Bone Marrow Transplants

For Hodgkin's patients who have not responded well to chemotherapy, radiation, or other standard forms of therapy, there is an additional option. The immune system can be boosted in other ways, as well. Stem cell and bone marrow transplants can replace the blood cells that are destroyed by chemotherapy and other treatments. Blood cells are made in bone marrow. The cells in the marrow that make blood are called stem cells. In addition to the marrow, stem cells are also present in peripheral blood, which is blood that flows in other parts of the body, and blood found in the umbilical cord or the placenta, after a baby is born.

Since doctors now have the ability to harvest these stem cells directly from the blood, it is not quite as difficult to harvest these cells as it once was. Compared to other blood cells, stem cells are much fewer in number. After these cells are harvested from the body, they are treated with drugs that increase the number

A surgeon removing bone marrow from a Hodgkin's lymphoma patient. This marrow will be treated to remove cancer cells and then returned to the patient's body in order to boost the person's immune system.

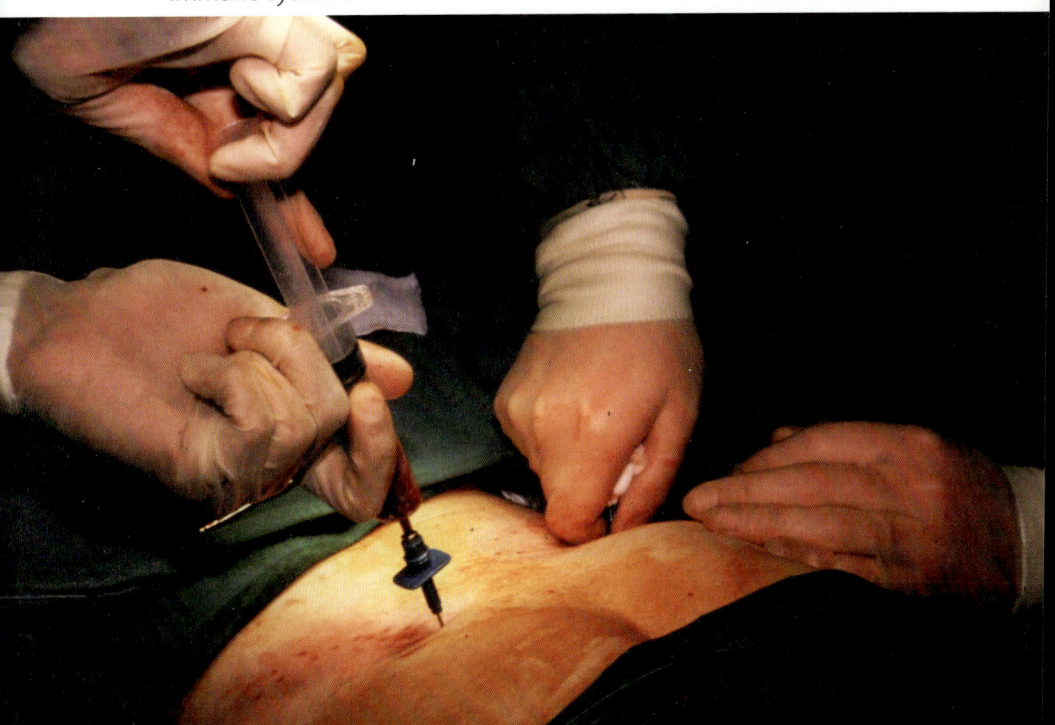

of stem cells. Since stem cells are more rare than other types of blood cells, a device called a hemapheresis machine circulates a large amount of blood and skims off the stem cells.

Sometimes, stem cells are taken from close family members or others whose blood closely matches the patient's. In the case of Hodgkin's lymphoma, though, stem cells are usually taken from the patient's own bone marrow. This is called autologous transplantation, or high dose therapy. The marrow is removed while the patient is in remission, treated with either chemotherapy drugs or monoclonal antibodies, and then returned to the patient's body. This process cleanses the marrow of any cancer cells that might be hiding in the marrow.

One lymphoma patient, a teenaged boy, described his experience with a stem cell transplant procedure when it was still in study stages, "I didn't think that I really had anything to lose doing a study. So, I went on with it, and it's worked great so far."[12] His doctor commented on the goal of the transplant procedure, "What we want to do is tilt the balance in favor of the immune system and away from the tumor or lymphoma."[13]

There are risks and side effects with this procedure as there are with any of the others. Since this procedure involves wiping other antibodies out of the body and replacing them with supercharged antibodies, the patient's overall health is at risk. Patient's undergoing this procedure should be as physically fit as possible. Additionally, the patient may experience such side effects as fatigue, loss of appetite, nausea, and vomiting. Some people also experience stiffness, cramps, and joint pain after stem cell transplants and for people of child-bearing age, there is some risk of infertility.

Stem cell transplant patients also run the risk of infection because their immune systems have been temporarily affected. Something as simple as a head cold or a sore throat is a potential danger for someone recovering from this procedure. Because of this, people who have had stem cell transplants need to avoid crowds and places where crowds gather during their recovery period. The number of weeks or months involved will be determined by the individual patient's medical team.

## Today's Cutting Edge and Looking Ahead

Again, though, issues such as side effects and recovery time vary with the individual. The patient's age and overall level of physical fitness are contributing factors, as well. One patient cannot measure his or her progress against that of another patient.

### Clinical Trials

A clinical trial is a process in which a medication or a treatment is tested to see if it is safe and effective. Clinical trials are usually the last step before drugs or treatments are approved for general medical use. Drugs being considered are tested extensively in laboratories for up to six years before they advance to clinical trials. On average, about one thousand drugs are tested for every drug that is finally approved.

Finally, the clinical trials themselves can go on for several years, because it takes years to determine if a drug actually does what it was created or modified to do. Another issue that can affect a clinical trial program is that sometimes there are

Two researchers performing tests on a possible cancer treatment in April 2007. It may take up to six years of testing in a laboratory before a drug is ready to move on to a clinical trial.

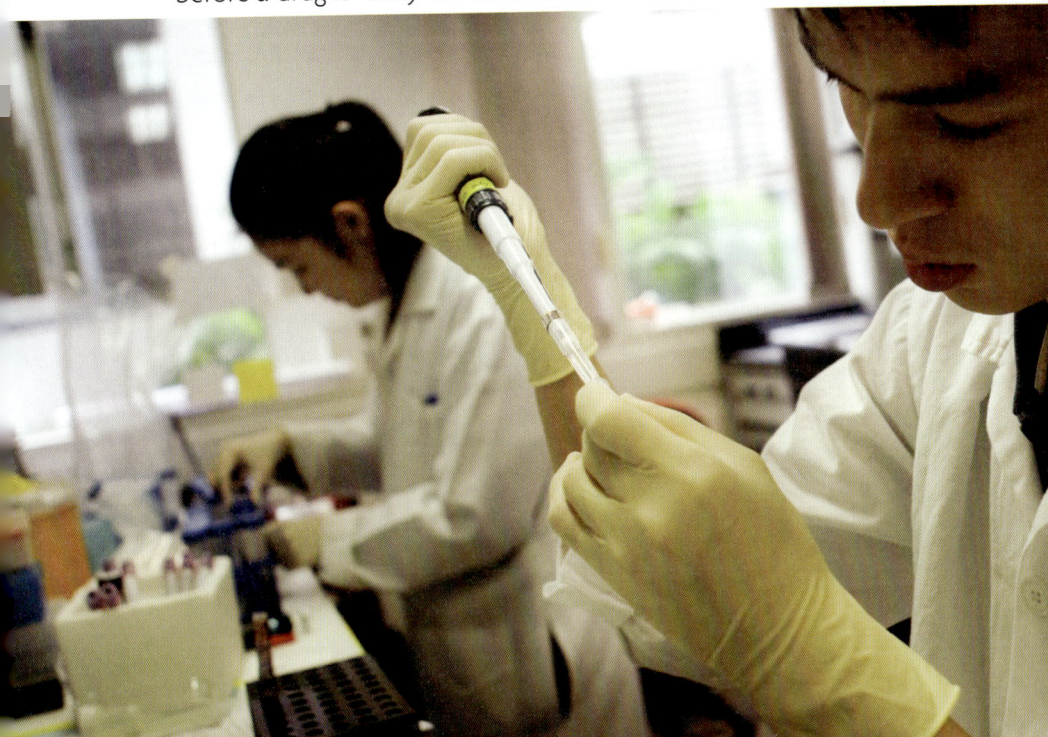

not enough volunteers to successfully conduct the program. Most clinical trials require a minimum number of participants. Otherwise, the study results will not give a realistic picture of how large numbers of people in treatment programs throughout the world might react to the drugs.

The shortage of volunteers for clinical trials may be due to the serious choices patients have to make regarding their treatment. If a person is thinking about entering a clinical trial, there are a number of things to keep in mind. First and foremost, the trial should be discussed with the patient's medical team to determine if it is the best type of trial for the person's particular medical needs. Also, the patient or the family should learn how much is known about the drug or combination of drugs in the trial.

Some people fear clinical trials because they think they will be treated like guinea pigs, little more than experimental

## Clinical Trials Cooperative Group Program

Many successful drugs and treatments have been developed through clinical trials. One program oversees thousands of these clinical trials every year. Sponsored by the National Cancer Institute, the Clinical Trials Cooperative Group Program was established in 1955. This program promotes and supports research studies related to cancer treatments, early detection and prevention of cancer, and treatment and post treatment rehabilitation.

By 1958, seventeen cooperative groups were involved with the center. Today, more than 1,700 facilities participate in the program. These facilities involve over 22,000 new patients in clinical trials every year. Information about the clinical trials currently underway and clinical trial enrollment can be obtained from the Cancer Information Services at 1-800-CANCER.

animals. They believe they will be seen as a set of symptoms, rather than human beings. Some fear that the trials are not safe or that their health insurance will not cover them.

However, there are a number of benefits for people participating in clinical trials. According to the National Cancer Institute, most clinical trial patients get the best of care with closer monitoring. They may also have access to the latest drugs and treatment programs not available to patients involved in standard treatment. Also, many insurance companies will cover all or part of the costs of some clinical trials, and some trials do not cost the patient anything, at all.

One clinical study for Hodgkin's lymphoma recently published its results. The study involved safely combining field radiation therapy with low-intensity chemotherapy in giving Hodgkin's disease a one-two punch. The study focused on the concern that combining high-dose chemotherapy with radiation can lead to serious long-term side effects, including lung problems, sterility, secondary cancers, and heart disease. The goal was to reduce these side effects.

Patients were divided into two groups. One group was given radiation therapy to the neck, chest, and lymph nodes under the arms, abdomen, and pelvis. The second group received the experimental low intensity four-drug chemotherapy followed by radiation that was directed only to the parts of the body where lymphoma was known to be present. This is called involved-field radiation therapy. With radiation limited to the disease-involved areas, healthy organs were better protected from the toxic effects of radiation. This approach carries a lower risk of developing secondary cancers in later years. Upon follow-up with these patients, the survival rate was about 90 percent, which is encouraging results for medical teams and future patients.

## The Future

Gene therapy is one therapy area for the treatment of Hodgkin's disease currently being clinically tested on a small scale. By definition, gene therapy is the implanting of new genetic material into a cell for therapeutic improvement. At this time,

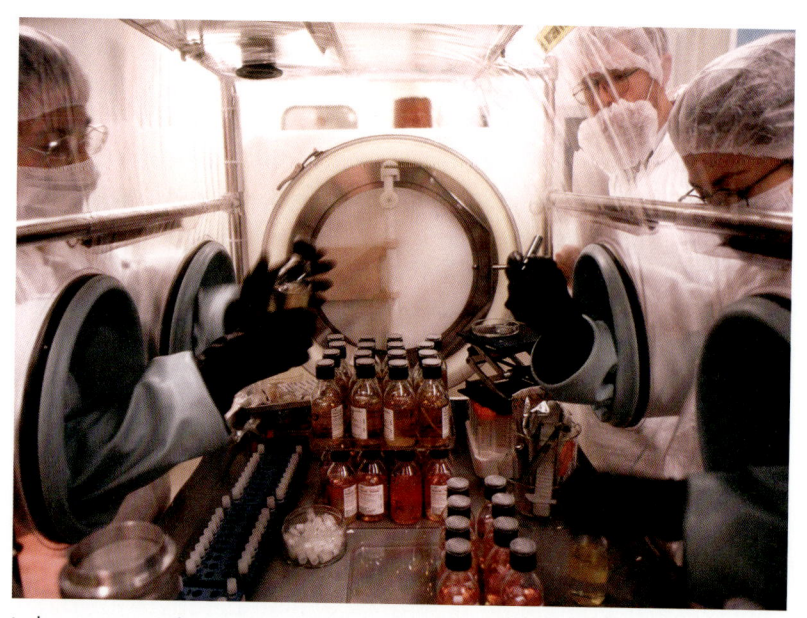

Laboratory technicians work with culture boxes used in gene therapy. Researchers are hoping that gene therapy will become an approved treatment for Hodgkin's lymphoma.

there are no gene therapies approved for the treatment of Hodgkin's lymphoma. However, gene therapy is being pursued as a way to control the rapid growth of cancer cells and to interact with the immune system in killing cancer cells. At this time, a few studies are being conducted with lymphoma patients in later stages of the disease. If the results are successful, these gene therapies will be ready for testing on patients in earlier stages.

Thanks to gene therapy, immunotherapy, and new developments in standard treatments, the future is brighter today than ever before for Hodgkin's patients. At one time, Hodgkin's and other types of cancer meant certain death. Today, though, many cancer treatments have brought patients up to 80 and 90 percent survival rates and even higher.

One important fact for Hodgkin's patients and their families to remember as they work through the treatment process is that the patient is a person first, with the same talents, likes, and dislikes that he or she had before the diagnosis and will

# DNA Mapping

Researchers are using human DNA to determine if a person is likely to develop serious illnesses. One of the main diseases being examined in DNA mapping research is cancer. By studying hundreds of DNA samples, tiny common patterns began to emerge. Haplotypes are tiny pieces of genetic information that help provide these genetic patterns. Some day in the future, scientists predict they will be able to use these patterns to determine early in a person's life if that individual is at risk of developing cancer, even years later. If so, the person can be placed on drugs to prevent the development or growth of cancer. Some people believe that DNA mapping is the key to curing Hodgkin's disease as well as other forms of cancer.

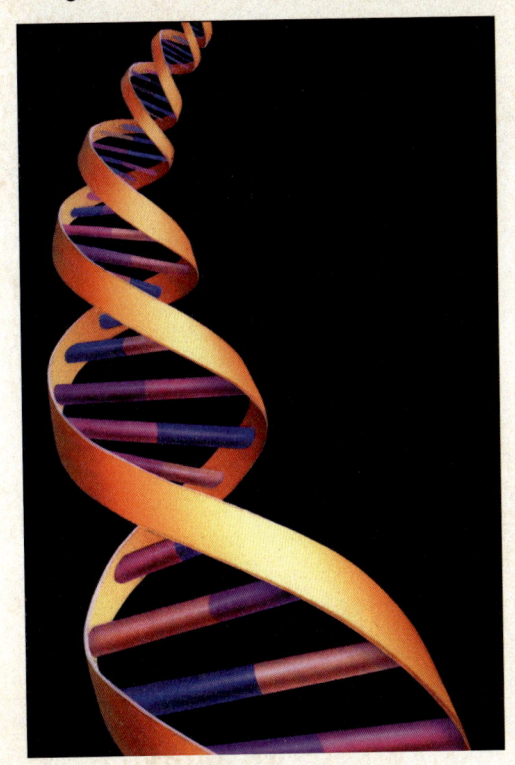

Scientists are using DNA samples, similar to this illustration, to research if there are genetic patterns that occur in people who develop Hodgkin's disease.

have long after the disease is cured. Writer Maureen McHugh did not let Hodgkin's define her life when she was in treatment, and does not allow it to do so now. She said,

> People say I was strong when I had Hodgkin's, but the truth is, for most of us, Hodgkin's is something we get, then we get cured of it. Hodgkin's is not fun. For some people, it's fatal. But I responded well to treatment and I've been fine since I finished. Hodgkin's, for the most part, did not change my life.[14]

# Notes

## Introduction: Naming a Nightmare
1. Maureen McHugh, quoted with permission, August 2007. "How I Learned I Have Hodgkin's." *No Feeling of Falling.* December 12, 2004. http://maureenmcg.blogspot.com/2004_12_01_archive.html.
2. Peter Mauch, Lawrence Weiss, and James O. Armitage. "Hodgkin's Disease," in *Cancer Medicine*, ed. Donald W. Kufe, et al. Hamilton, Ont., Canada: B.C. Decker, 2003.

## Chapter 1: What is Hodgkin's Disease?
3. Quoted in the *Internet Journal of Advanced Nursing Practice*, "Lymphadenopathy in Hodgkin's Disease of the Nodular Sclerosing Subtype: Case Presentation." www.ispub.com/ostia/index.php?xmlFilePath=journals/ijanp/vol4n1/lymph.xml.
4. Quoted in American Association for Cancer Research, "Prognosis: Predicting Cancer Risk in the Long-Term," *aacr.org*, April 16, 2007. www.aacr.org/home/public==media/news/news=archives=2007.aspx?d=739.

## Chapter 2: Diagnosing Hodgkin's Disease
5. Quoted in Toni L. Rocha, *Someone in Your Family Has Cancer.* New York: The Rosen Group, 2001, p.11.

## Chapter 3: Treatments
6. Maureen McHugh, "Denial, it's Not Just a River in Egypt," *No Feeling of Falling*, January 15, 2005. http://maureenmcg.blogspot.com/2005_01_01_archive.html.

## Chapter 4: Alternative Therapies
7. Evelyn Reynolds, quoted with permission, August 2007. From author interview.

8. Dr. Anna L. Schwartz, *Cancer Fitness*. New York: Simon & Schuster, 2004, p. 166.
9. Emile Coue, "Visualisation Therapy," *New Choices*, 2003–2004. www.cocaine-addiction.co.uk/visualisation_therapy.htm.

## Chapter 5: Living and Coping
10. Rami Gafni, *Beauty Therapy*. New York: M. Evans and Company, 2005, p. 18.
11. Quoted in Rocha, *Someone in Your Family Has Cancer*, p. 65.

## Chapter 6: Today's Cutting Edge and Looking Ahead
12. Quoted in WCHS ABC 8, "Reviving the Immune System: Healthy for Life," 2008. www.wchstv.com/newsroom/healthyforlife/2088.shtml.
13. Quoted in "Reviving the Immune System: Healthy for Life."
14. Maureen McHugh, quoted with permission, August 2007. From author interview.

# Glossary

**ABVD:** The abbreviated name for one group of drugs used in chemotherapy for Hodgkin's disease.
**antibodies:** Y-shaped protein molecules that work with the body's immune system.
**antigens:** Toxins, bacteria, and other foreign substances that stimulate the production of antibodies in the body.
**biopsy:** Removing a tissue sample from a person's body in order to help make a diagnosis.
**bracytherapy:** A type of radiotherapy in which the source of radiation is placed close to or inside the body.
**chemotherapy:** Treating various types of cancer with chemicals that are toxic to the cancer cells.
**Complementary and Alternative Medicine:** Also called CAM therapies, the use of nontraditional treatments in addition to or in place of conventional medicine.
**Computed Tomography (CT):** A three-dimensional image of the body constructed using X-rays and computer technology.
**cytokine:** Proteins released by cells in the immune system.
**DNA:** Deoxyribonucleic acid, the material that is responsible for genetic characteristics of all life-forms.
**External Beam Radiation:** Using high-energy X-rays to destroy or slow the growth of cancer cells.
**gallium scan:** A nuclear medicine test that uses a specially designed camera to take pictures of body tissues after the patient ingests a radioactive material to make the tissues and organs more visible.
**gene therapy:** Using genetic engineering to transplant genes in an effort to cure disease.
**hemaphoresis machine:** A machine that separates blood into its components.
**Hodgkin's disease:** A cancer of the lymphatic system.

**immunotherapy:** Treatments designed to strengthen the immune system and fight disease.
**intravenous injection:** Injecting a substance into a vein.
**lacunar cells:** Cells with empty space around the nucleus.
**laparotomy:** An incision through the abdominal wall.
**lymph node:** Gland-like masses of tissue located in the lymphatic tissues of the armpits, neck, or groin area.
**lymphangiogram:** Procedure in which a contrast material is injected into the body and lymph glands are then X-rayed.
**lymphocytes:** Colorless cells found in blood and lymphatic tissue that accounts for about 25 percent of the white blood cells in the body.
**Magnetic Resonance Imaging (MRI):** A noninvasive procedure that creates sectional images of internal organs.
**malignant:** An uncontrolled growth of cancer cells.
**neuropathy:** A disease of the nervous system. One symptom of this condition is numbness in hands and feet.
**nitrogen mustard:** A poisonous substance once used in chemical warfare that has been effective in chemotherapy treatment.
**oncologist:** A doctor who treats different types of cancer.
**Positron Emission Tomography (PET):** A cross-sectional image of part of the body.
**prophylactic vaccine:** A vaccine that prevents disease.
**Reed-Sternberg cells:** Giant cells associated with Hodgkin's disease.
**stem cells:** Primal cells that have the ability to develop into many different types of cells found in the body.
**T-cells:** White blood cells that are a part of the body's immune system.
**Unsealed Source Radiotherapy:** One type of radiation therapy in which radioactive material is placed inside the body.
**VAMP:** Acronym for a group of drugs used in chemotherapy.

# Organizations to Contact

### American Cancer Society
1599 Clifton Rd. NE, Atlanta, GA 30329
(800) 227-2345
www.cancer.org

This organization provides information and support for Hodgkin's patients and their families.

### Leukemia and Lymphoma Society
1311 Mamaroneck Ave., White Plains, NY 10605
(914) 949-5213
www.leukemia-lymphoma.org/hm_lls

The Leukemia and Lymphoma Society provides information on patient services, support groups in different parts of the country, and information on financial support.

### National Children's Cancer Society
1015 Locust, Suite 600, St. Louis, MO 63101
(314) 241-1600
e-mail: krudd@children-cancer.org
www.nationalchildrenscancersociety.com

This organization provides support information for young cancer patients and their families as well as information about financial assistance.

## Ronald McDonald House Charities
One Kroc Dr., Oak Brook, IL 60523
(630) 623-7048
http://rmhc.org/rmhc/indcx.html

The Ronald McDonald House Charities provides low cost or free housing to families of young cancer patients as well has home-like get-aways on the hospital premises.

# For Further Reading

## Books

Ramy Gafni, *Beauty Therapy*. New York: M. Evans and Company, 2005. Information about wigs, head coverings, skin care, and makeup for cancer patients.

Lisa Hoffman with Alison Freeland, *The Healing Power of Movement*. Cambridge, MA: Perseus Publishing, 2002. Explains the benefits of exercise and different levels of exercise cancer patients can perform during various phases of their treatment.

Terry Priestman, *Coping with Chemotherapy*. London: Sheldon Press, 2005. Describes chemotherapy, side effects, and how to cope with them.

Toni L. Rocha, *Someone in Your Family Has Cancer*. New York: Rosen Publishing, 2001. Describes how to overcome fears and interacting with family members who have cancer. Also includes support group information.

Anna L. Schwartz, Ph D, *Cancer Fitness*. New York: Simon & Schuster, 2004. Explains how exercise can aid in cancer recovery and overall mental and physical wellbeing.

## Web Sites

**American Cancer Society.** www.cancer.org.
This web site provides educational information about all types of cancer, including Hodgkin's disease. Also provides information about healthy lifestyles and links to support programs and groups.

**HowStuffWorks, Inc.,** "How Stuff Works." www.howstuffworks.com.
This web site describes MRI, PET scans, and CT.

**The Leukemia and Lymphoma Society.** www.leukemia-lymphoma.org/hm_lls.

This web site provides information about patient services, basic information about Hodgkin's disease and leukemia, and includes the latest research information.

**Ronald McDonald House Charities.** http://rmhc.org/rmhc/index.html.

This is the official web site describing all of the Ronald McDonald Charities, including Ronald McDonald House, where family members of young patients may stay while their loved ones are having treatment, and Ronald McDonald Family Rooms, home-like spaces within the hospital for patients and their families.

# Index

ABVD drug combination, 42, 45
Acupuncture, 56
Alternative therapies, 52–64
   exercise, 59–63
   nutrition, 57–59
   overview, 52, 54
   visualization therapy, 63–64
   *See also* specific alternative therapies
American Cancer Society, 75
American Medical Association, 56
Antibodies, 78–79
Aromatherapy, 55–56
Ayurvedic medicine, 53 *53*

Barrett, Stephen, 54
*Beauty Therapy* (Gafni), 65–66
Bed and chair exercise, 63
Biological Response Modifiers (BRMs), 79–80
Biological therapy, 79–80
Biopsies, 33–37
Blood tests, 29
Bone marrow biopsy, 34
Bone marrow transplants, *81*, 81–83
Brachytherapy, 47–48, 49
Bright, Richard, 10
BRMs (Biological Response Modifiers), 79–80

CAM (complementary and alternative medicine). *See* Complementary and alternative medicine (CAM)
Cancer "cures." *See Quackwatch* (website)
*Cancer Fitness* (Schwartz), 61
CG DNA, 79
Chemotherapy, 39, *40*, 41–44, 45
   ABVD drug combination, 45
   cytotoxicity, 39, 41
   history, 41, *44*
   injection, 41
   IV (intravenous injection), 40, 41, 42
   oral, 41
   side effects, 42–43, 57, 66, 67
Clinical trials, *83*, 83–85
Clinical Trials Cooperative Group Program, 84
Complementary and alternative medicine (CAM)
   acupuncture, 56–57
   aromatherapy, 55–56
   conventional therapies v., 55
   exercise, 59, *60*, 61–63
   massage, *54*
   nutritional, 53
   overview, 52, 54–55
   visualization and meditation, 63–64
Contrast materials, 31, 32

Conventional therapies,
    39–51
  chemotherapy, 39, *40*,
    41–44, 45
  drugs, 50–51
  overview, 39
  radiation, 45, 47–50
Coping (with Hodgkin's
    disease)
  overview, 65
  self-image and physical
    changes, 65–67
  self-image support, *66*,
    66–71, 69, 70
  support groups and
    organizations, *72*
Core biopsy, 34
Coue, Emile, 63
CT scan (computed tomography scan), 30–31
"Cures" for cancer. *See
    Quackwatch* (website)
Cytokine therapy, 80
Cytoplasm, 16–17

Diagnosis, 26–38
  biopsies, 33–37
  blood tests, 29
  imaging device tests, 29–33
  overview, 26–27
  physical examination and
    medical history, 27–29
Diet, 57, 57–59
DNA mapping, 87
DNA-related experimental
  medications, 79
Drugs, 50–51
  *See also* Clinical trials

EBRT (external beam radiotherapy), 47–48
Epoetin, 51, *51*

Excisional biopsy, 37–38
Exercise, 59–63
  bed and chair, 63
  goals, 61–62
  walking, *60*, 61
  yoga, 62–63
Experimental treatments. *See*
  Research
Exploratory surgery, 37–38
External beam radiotherapy
  (EBRT), 47–48

*Fantastic Voyage* (movie),
  77, *78*
Fine needle aspiration (FNA),
  33–34

Gafni, Rami, 65–66
Gallium scan, 31–32
Gattefosse, Rene Maurice, 56
Gene therapy, 85–86, *86*, *87*
Greenfield, W.S., 11

History, 9–13, *12*
Hodgkin, Thomas, 9–10, *9*
Hodgkin's disease
  age prevalence, 14
  alternative therapies, 52–63
  children, 22, 23–25
  conventional therapies,
    39–51
  history, 10
  impact on family, 71–74
  medications, 50–51
  monitoring, 20
  physical appearance
    changes, 65–67, 69
  progressive nature, 15
  research and future treatment possibilities, 77–88
  side effects, 21, 24–25,
    50–51

# Index

stages, 19–20, 22, 23
statistics, 14, 16, 17, 18–19
support groups and organizations, 74, 75–76
symptoms, 18–19, *19*, 20, 21, 23–25, 27–28
types, 16–19
*See also* Diagnosis; specific research projects and treatment possibilities; specific therapies
Hodgkin's lymphoma. *See* Hodgkin's disease

Imaging devices, 29–33
Immune system research and therapies, 78–80
Immunotherapy, 79–80
Integrated medicine. *See* Complementary and alternative medicine (CAM)
Intravenous dye, 31
Intravenous injection (IV), 30
*See also* Chemotherapy

Kaplan, Harry S., 21
Kim's Place, 22
Kytril, 51

L & H (lymphocytic and histolytic) cells, 18
Lacunar cells, 16
Laparotomy, 37–38
Large needle biopsy, 34
Leukemia and Lymphoma Society, 56
Leukocytes, 58–59
Linear accelerator, 21
Living (with Hodgkin's disease). *See* Coping (with Hodgkin's disease)

Locks of Love, 71
LSF (Lymphoma Support Foundation), 75
Lymphangiogram, 32–33
Lymphatic system, 14–15, *15*
Lymphocyte depletion, 17
Lymphocyte-rich classical Hodgkin's lymphoma, 18
Lymphocytes, 15
Lymphocytic and histolytic (L&H) cells, 18
Lymphoma Support Foundation (LSF), 75

Macrobiotic diet, 58–59
Magnetic resonance tomography (MRI), *30*, 31
Mantle field, 48–49
Massage therapy, *54*, 55
McHugh, Maureen, 8, 43, 88
Medication, 50–51
*See also* Clinical trials
Meditation, 63–64
Mixed cellularity, 16, *16*, 17
Monoclonal antibodies, 80
MRI (magnetic resonance tomography), *30*, 31

National Cancer Institute, 84, 85
National Center for Complementary and Alternative Medicine (NCCAM), 56–57
National Institute of Health (NIH), 56–57
NCCAM (National Center for Complementary and Alternative Medicine), 56–57
NIH (National Institute of Health), 56–57

Nitrogen mustard, *41*, 41, 44
Nodular lymphocyte predominance, 17–18
Nodular sclerosis, *16*, 16–17
Non-Hodgkin's lymphoma, 14
Nutrition, *57*, 57–59

Pathologist, 33
PET scan (positron emission tomography scan), 32
Physical examinations, 28–29
Physical therapy, 35
Popcorn cells, 18
Positron emission tomography (PET) scan, 32
Procrit, *51*, 51

Quackery, 62
*Quackwatch* (website), 54

Radiation oncologist, 48
Radiation therapy, 45–50, *48*
　chemotherapy combination, 47
　chemotherapy v., 45
　early efforts, 11, *12*, 13
　effect, 45
　history, 45, 46
　imaging device tests, 47
　lymphoma location, 48–49
　medications, *51*
　side effects, 50, 57
　treatment ports, 48, 49
　types, 47–48
Radioactive seed implants, 49
Radioactive substances, 31–32
Radiocontrast, 31
Radiotherapy.
　*See* Radiation therapy

Reed, Dorothy, 11
Reed-Sternberg cells, 14, *16*, 18, 33
Remote site surgery, 77–78
Research, 77–86
　clinical trials, 83–85
　DNA mapping, 87, *87*
　gene therapy, 85–86
　immunotherapy, 78–80
　overview, 77–78
　stem cell transplants, 81–83
Roentgen, Wilhelm, 45, *46*
Ronald McDonald House Charities, 22, 76
Rosenberg, Saul, 21

Schwartz, Anna, 61
Sealed source radiotherapy, 47–48
Sibling Support Project, 75
Spleen, *37*, 37–38
Splenectomy, 37–38
Staging process, 19
Stem cell transplants, 81–83
Sternberg, Carl, 11
Stroke, *24*
Support groups and organizations, 74, 75–76
Surgery, 34–36, 37–38
　*See also* Exploratory surgery; Surgical biopsy
Surgical biopsy, 34–35, 37

T-cell immunotherapy, 80
Telerobotics, 78
Teletherapy, 47–48
Testing devices, 29–33
Tests. *See* Diagnosis
Total nodal irradiation, 48–49
Treatments. *See* Alternative therapies; Conventional therapies; specific therapies

# Index

Unsealed source radiotherapy, 47–48

Vaccine therapy, 80
Visualization and Meditation, 63–64
"Visualization Therapy" (Coue), 63

Wilks, Samuel, 10–11

X-ray, 30
X-ray therapy. *See* Radiation therapy

Yoga, 62–63

Zofran, 51

# Picture Credits

Cover: © Lester V. Bergman/Corbis
AP Images, 54, 60, 66, 83
Alfred Pasieka/Photo Researchers, Inc., 37
© Bettmann/Corbis, 12
BSIP/Photo Researchers, Inc., 72
Burger/Photo Researchers, Inc., 40
Centre Oscar Lambret/Photo Researchers, Inc., 48
Custom Medical Stock Photo, Inc. Reproduced by permission, 36, 51
Dr. Dorothea Zucker-Franklin/Phototake. Reproduced by permission., 16
Dr. Rob Stepney/Photo Researchers, 81
Dr. Tim Evans/Photo Researchers, Inc., 44
Erik Hildebrandt/Photo Researchers, Inc., 21
Frank Siteman/Science Faction/Getty Images, 27
Juan Silva/The Image Bank/Getty Images, 69, 70
Kerry Wetzel/Photographer's Choice/Getty Images, 57
© NMSB/Custom Medical Stock Photo, 19
Nucleus Medical Art, Inc./Phototake. reproduced by permission, 24, 33
© Peter Widmann/Alamy, 30
Phanie/Photo Researchers, Inc., 86
Renate Forster/StockFood Creative/Getty Images, 53
Science Source/Photo Researchers, Inc., 46
SPL/Photo Researchers, Inc., 9
T. Buck/Custom Medical Stock Photo, 87
20th Century Fox Film Corp. All rights reserved. Courtesy Everett Collection 78
© Visuals Unlimited/Corbis, 15

# About the Author

Sheila Wyborny has been writing books for children and young adults since she retired from the classroom. She and her husband, Wendell, an engineer, live in an airport community near Houston, Texas. They share their home with four birds and their Cessna 170 airplane, Lucy.